MR. FORTUNE'S
MAGGOT

By the same author

LOLLY WILLOWES
OR THE LOVING
HUNTSMAN

1926

MR. FORTUNE'S MAGGOT

"MAGGOT 2. A nonsensical or perverse fancy; a crotchet." N.E.D.

By

SYLVIA TOWNSEND
WARNER

NEW YORK
THE LITERARY GUILD
OF AMERICA
1927

100496

Printed in the United States of America

Copyright, 1927, by

THE VIKING PRESS, INC.

To
THEO

THE SCENES AND CHARACTERS of this story are entirely imaginary. In the island names the vowels should be pronounced separately with the Italianate vowel-sounds. Words of three syllables are accented on the second: Fanùa, Luèli.

I am greatly obliged to Mr. Victor Butler for his assistance in the geometrical passages, and for the definition of an umbrella.

MR. FORTUNE'S
MAGGOT

THOUGH, the Reverend Timothy Fortune had spent three years in the island of Fanua he had made but one convert. Some missionaries might have been galled by this state of things, or if too good to be galled, at least flustered; but Mr. Fortune was a humble man of heart and he had the blessing which rests upon humility: an easy-going nature. In appearance he was tall, raw-boned and rather rummaged looking; even as a young man he had learnt that to jump in first doesn't make the bus start any sooner; and his favourite psalm was the one which begins: My soul truly waiteth still upon God.

Mr. Fortune was not a scholar, he did not know that the psalms express bygone thoughts and a bygone way of life. In his literal way he believed that the sixty-second psalm applied to him. For many years he had been a clerk in the Hornsey branch of Lloyds Bank, but he had not liked it. Whenever he weighed out the golden sovereigns in the brass scales which tacked and sidled like a yacht in a light breeze he remembered uneasily that the children of men are deceitful upon the weights, that they are altogether lighter than vanity itself.

In the bank too he had seen riches increase. But he had not set his heart upon them; and when his godmother, whose pass-book he kept, died and left him one thousand pounds he went to a training college, was ordained deacon, and quitted England for St. Fabien, a port on an island of the Raritongan Archipelago in the Pacific.

St. Fabien was a centre of Christianity. It had four missions: one Catholic, one Protestant, one Wesleyan, and one American. Mr. Fortune belonged to the Protestant mission. He gave great satisfaction to his superiors by doing as he was bid, teaching in the school, visiting the sick, and carrying the subscription list to the English visitors, and even greater satisfaction when they had discovered that he could keep all the accounts. At the end of ten years Archdeacon Mason was sorry to hear that Mr. Fortune (who was now a priest) had felt a call to go to the island of Fanua.

Fanua was a small remote island which could only be seen in imagination from that beach edged with tin huts where Mr. Fortune walked slowly up and down on evenings when he had time to. No steamers called there, the archdeacon had visited it many years ago in a canoe. Now his assistant felt a call thither, not merely to visit it in the new mission launch, but to settle there, and perhaps for life.

The two clergymen strolled along the beach in the cool of the evening. The air smelt of the sea, of flowers, and of the islanders' suppers.

"I must warn you, Fortune, you are not likely to make many converts in Fanua."

"What, are they cannibals?"

"No, no! But they are like children, always singing and dancing, and of course immoral. But all the natives are like that. I believe I have told you that the Raritongan language has no word for chastity or for gratitude?"

"Yes, I believe you did."

"Well, well! You are not a young man, Fortune, you will not expect too much of the Fanuans. Singing and dancing! No actual harm in that of course, and no doubt the climate is partly responsible. But light, my dear Fortune, light! And not only in their heels either."

3

"I am afraid that none of the children of men weigh altogether true," said Mr. Fortune. "For that matter I have heard that many cannibals are fond of dancing."

"Humanly speaking I fear that you would be wasted in Fanua. Still, if you have felt a call I must not dissuade you, I won't put any obstacles in your way. But you will be a great loss."

The Archdeacon spoke so sadly that Mr. Fortune, knowing how much he disliked accounts, wondered for a moment if God would prefer him to wait still in St. Fabien. God tries the souls of men in crafty ways and perhaps the call had been a temptation, a temptation sent to try his humility. He turned his eyes towards where he knew the island of Fanua to lie. What his superior had said about it had not displeased him, on the contrary he liked to think of the islanders dancing and singing. It would be a beautiful estate to live among them and gather their souls as a child gathers daisies in a field.

But now the horizon was hidden in the evening haze, and Fanua seemed more remote than ever. A little cloud was coming up the heavens, slowly, towards the sunset; as it passed above the place of Fanua it brightened, it shone like a

pearl, it caught the rays of the sun and glowed
with a rosy rim. Mr. Fortune took the cloud to
be a sign.

Heartened by a novel certainty that he was
doing the right thing he disappointed the Archdeacon quite unflinchingly, and set about his
preparations for the new life. Since the island
was so unfrequented it was necessary to take
with him provisions for at least a year. In the
ordinary course of things the Mission would
have supplied his outfit, but he had a scruple
against availing himself of this custom, because having kept the accounts he knew their
poverty and their good works, and also he was
aware that the expedition to Fanua was looked
on as, at best, a sort of pious escapade. Fortunately there was the remains of his godmother's
legacy. With feelings that were a nice mixture
of thrift and extravagance he bought tinned
meats, soup-squares, a chest of tea, soap, a tool-
box, a medicine chest, a gentleman's housewife,
a second-hand harmonium (rather cumbrous and
wheezy but certainly a bargain) and an oil-
lamp. He also bought a quantity of those coloured glass baubles which hang so ravishingly
on Christmas trees, some picture-books, rolls of
white cotton, and a sewing-machine to make

clothes for his converts. The Archdeacon gave
him a service of altar furniture and the other
mission-workers presented him with a silver tea-
pot. With the addition of some plate-powder
Mr. Fortune was now ready to embark.

In fancy he had seen himself setting foot
upon the island alone though he knew that in
fact someone must go with him if only to manage the launch. But that someone would be a
sailor, a being so aloofly maritime as scarcely to
partake in the act of landing. He was slightly
dashed when he discovered that the Archdeacon,
accompanied by his secretary, was coming too
in order to install him with a proper appearance
of ceremony.

"We cannot impress upon them too early,"
said the Archdeacon, "the solemn nature of
your undertaking." And Mr. Fortune hung his
head, a grey one, old and wise enough to heed
an admonition or a rebuke.

The voyage was uneventful. The Archdeacon sat in the bows dictating to the secretary,
and Mr. Fortune looked at the Pacific Ocean
until he fell asleep, for he was tired out with
packing.

About sunset he was aroused by the noise of
surf and by peals of excited laughter; and open-

ing his eyes he found that they were close in under the shadow of the island of Fanua. The launch was manœuvring round seeking for an inlet in the reef, and the islanders were gathered together to view this strange apparition. Some were standing on the rocks, some were in the sea, others were diving from cliff to water, in movement and uproar like a flock of sea-gulls disturbed by a fishing-boat.

It seemed to Mr. Fortune that there must be thousands of them, and for a moment his heart sank. But there was no time for second thoughts; for behold! a canoe shot forward to the side of the launch, a rope was thrown and caught, the Archdeacon, the secretary and himself were miraculously jumped in, the sea was alive with brown heads, everyone talked at once, the canoe turned, darted up the smooth back of a wave, descended into a cloud of spray, and the three clergymen, splashed and stiff, were standing on the beach.

Now Mr. Fortune was properly grateful for the presence of the Archdeacon, for like a child arriving late at a party he felt perfectly bewildered and would have remained in the same spot, smiling and staring. But like the child at the party he found himself taken charge of and

7

shepherded in the right direction until, in the house of the chief islander, he was seated on a low stool with his hat taken off, a garland round his neck and food in his hands, smiling and staring still.

Before dark the luggage was also landed. The evening was spent in conversation and feasting. Everyone who could squeeze himself into Ori's house did so, and the rest of them (the thousands did not seem above a few hundreds now) squatted round outside. Even the babies seemed prepared to sit there all night, but at length the Archdeacon, pleading fatigue, asked leave of his host to go to bed.

Ori dismissed the visitors, his household prepared the strangers' sleeping place, unrolling the best mats and shooing away a couple of flying foxes, the missionaries prayed together and the last good-nights were said.

From where he lay Mr. Fortune could look out of the door. He saw a tendril of some creeper waving gently to and fro across the star Canopus, and once more he realized, as though he were looking at it for the first time, how strangely and powerfully he had been led from his native land to lie down in peace under the constellations of the southern sky.

8

"So this is my first night in Fanua," he thought, as he settled himself on his mat. "My first night. . . ."

And he would have looked at the star, a sun whose planets must depend wholly upon God for their salvation, for no missionary could reach them; but his eyes were heavy with seafaring, and in another minute he had fallen asleep.

As though while his body lay sleeping his ghost had gone wandering and ascertaining through the island Mr. Fortune woke on the morrow feeling perfectly at home in Fanua. So much so that when he stood on the beach waving farewell to the launch he had the sensations of a host, who from seeing off his guests turns back with a renewed sense of ownership to the house which the fact of their departure makes more deeply and dearly his. Few hosts indeed could claim an ownership equally secure. For when the Archdeacon, visited with a sudden qualm at the thought of Mr. Fortune's isolation, had suggested that he should come again in three months' time, just to see how he was getting on, Mr. Fortune was able to say quite serenely and legitimately that he would prefer to be left alone for at least a year.

Having waved to the proper degree of perspective he turned briskly inland. The time was come to explore Fanua.

The island of Fanua is of volcanic origin, though at the time of Mr. Fortune's arrival the volcano had been for many years extinct. It rises steeply out of the ocean, and seen from thence it appears disproportionately tall for its base, for the main peak reaches to a height of near three thousand feet, and the extremely indented coast-line does not measure more than seventy miles. On three sides of the island there are steep cliffs worked into caverns and flying buttresses by the action of the waves, but to the east a fertile valley slopes gently down to a low-lying promontory of salt-meadow and beach where once a torrent of lava burst from the side of the mountain and crushed its channel to the sea; and in this valley lies the village.

The lower slopes of the mountain are wooded, and broken into many deep gorges where the noise of the cataract echoes from cliff to cliff, where the air is cool with shade and moist with spray, and where bright green ferns grow on the black face of the rock. Above this swirl and foam of tree-tops the mountain rises up in crags or steep tracts of scrub and clinker to the old crater, whose ramparts are broken into curi-

ous cactus-shaped pinnacles of rock, in colour
the reddish lavender of rhododendron blossoms.

A socket of molten stone, rent and deserted
by its ancient fires and garlanded round with a
vegetation as wild as fire and more inexhaustible, the whole island breathes the peculiar ro-
mance of a being with a stormy past. The ripened fruit falls from the tree, the tree falls too
and the ferns leap up from it as though it were
being consumed with green flames. The air is
sleepy with salt and honey, and the sharp wild
cries of the birds seem to float like fragments of
coloured paper upon the monotonous background
of breaking waves and falling cataract.

Mr. Fortune spent the whole day exploring,
and when he felt hungry he made a meal of
guavas and rose-apples. There seemed to be no
end to the marvels and delights of his island
and he was as thrilled as though he had been let
loose into the world for the first time. But he
returned with all the day's wonders almost forgotten in the excitement and satisfaction of having discovered the place where he wanted to
live.

It was a forsaken hut, about a mile from the
village and less than that distance from the sea.
It stood in a little dell amongst the woods; be-

fore it there was a natural lawn of fine grass, behind it was a rocky spur of the mountain. There was a spring for water and a clump of coco-palms for shade.

The hut consisted of one large room opening on to a deep verandah. The framework was of wood, the floor of beaten earth, and it was thatched and walled with reeds.

Ori told him that it could be his for the taking. An old woman had lived there with her daughter, but she had died and the daughter, who didn't like being out of the world, had removed to the village. Mr. Fortune immediately set about putting it in order, and while he worked almost everyone in the island dropped in at some time or other to admire, encourage or lend a hand. There was not much to do; a little strengthening of the thatch, the floor to be weeded and trodden smooth, the creepers to be cut back—and on the third day he moved in.

This took place with ceremony. The islanders accompanied him on his many journeys to and from the village, they carried the crate containing the harmonium with flattering eulogies of its weight and size, and when everything was transported they sat on the lawn and watched

12

him unpacking. When he unpacked the tea-pot they burst into delighted laughter.

Except for the lamp, the sewing machine and the harmonium Mr. Fortune's house had not an European appearance, for while on the island he wished to live as its natives did. His bowls and platters and drinking-vessels were made of polished wood, his bed (Ori's gift) was a small wooden platform spread with many white mats. When everything was completed he gave each of the islanders a ginger-bread nut and made a little formal speech, first thanking them for their gifts and their assistance, and going on to explain his reasons for coming to Fanua. He had heard, he said, with pleasure how happy a people they were, and he had come to dwell with them, and teach them how they might be as happy in another life as they were in this.

The islanders received his speech in silence, broken only by crunching. Their expressions were those of people struck into awe by some surprising novelty. Mr. Fortune wondered if he were that novelty, or Huntley and Palmer.

He was anxious to do things befittingly for the Archdeacon's admonition on the need for

13

being solemn still hung about the back of his mind. This occasion, it seemed to him, was something between a ceremony and a social function. It was a gathering, and as such it had its proper routine: first there comes an address, after the address a hymn is sung, then comes a collect and sometimes a collection and after that the congregation disperses.

Mr. Fortune sat down to his harmonium and sang and played through a hymn.

His back was to the islanders, he could not see how they were taking it. But when, having finished the hymn and added two chords for the Amen, he turned round to announce the collect he discovered that they had already dispersed, the last of them even then vanishing noiselessly and enigmatically through the bushes.

The sun was setting behind the mountain, great shafts of glory moved among the topmost crags. Mr. Fortune thought of God's winnowing-fan, he imagined Him holding the rays of the sun in His hand. God winnows the souls of men with the beauty of this world: the chaff is blown away, the true grain lies still and adoring.

In the dell it was already night. He sat for a long time in his verandah listening to the

boom of the waves. He did not think much, he
was tired with a long day's work and his back
ached. At last he went indoors, lighted his lamp
and began to write in his diary. Just as he was
dropping off to sleep a pleasant thought came to
him, and he smiled, murmuring in a drowsy
voice: "To-morrow is Sunday."

In the morning he was up and shaved and
dressed before sunrise. With a happy face he
stepped on to his lawn and stood listening to
the birds. They did not sing anywhere near so
sweetly as English blackbirds and thrushes, but
Mr. Fortune was pleased with their notes, a
music which seemed proper to this gay landscape
which might have been coloured out of a child's
paint box.

He stood there till the sun had risen and shone
into the dell, then he went back into his hut;
when he came out again he was dressed in his
priest's clothes and carried a black tin box.

He walked across the dell to where there was
a stone with a flat top. Opening the box he took
out, first a linen cloth which he spread on the
stone, then a wooden cross and two brass vases.
He knelt down and very carefully placed the
cross so that it stood firm on the middle of the
stone. The vases he carried to the spring where

he filled them with water, and gathering some red blossoms which grew on a bush near-by he arranged them in the vases, which he then carried back and set on either side of the cross. Standing beside the stone and looking into the sun, he said in a loud voice: "Let your light so shine before men that they may see your good works and glorify your Father which is in heaven."

The sun shone upon the white cloth and the scarlet flowers, upon the cross of wood and upon the priest standing serious, grey-headed and alone in the green dell all sparkling with dew as though it had never known the darkness of night.

Once more he turned and went back to the hut. When he came out again he carried in either hand a cup and a dish which shone like gold. These he put down upon the stone, and bowed himself before them and began to pray.

Mr. Fortune knelt very upright. His eyes were shut, he did not see the beauty of the landscape glittering in the sunrise, the coco-palms waving their green feather head-dresses gently to and fro in the light breeze, the wreaths of rosy mist floating high up across the purple crags

of the mountain; and yet from the expression
on his face one would have said that he was all
the more aware of the beauty around him for
having his eyes shut, for he seemed like one in
an ecstasy and his clasped hands trembled, as
though they had hold of a joy too great for
him. He knelt on, absorbed in prayer. He did
not see that a naked brown boy had come to
the edge of the dell, and was gazing at him,
and at the stone which he had decked to the
glory of God—gazing with wonder and admiration, and step by step coming softly across
the grass. Only when he had finished his prayer
and stretched out his hands towards the altar
did Mr. Fortune discover that a boy was kneeling at his side.

He gave no sign of surprise, he did not appear even to have noticed the newcomer. With
steadfast demeanour he took from the dish a
piece of bread and ate it, and drank from the
cup. Then, rising and turning to the boy who
still knelt before him, he laid his hand upon his
head, and looked down on him with a long look
of greeting. Slowly and unhesitatingly, like one
who hears and accepts and obeys the voice of the
spirit, he took up the cup once more and with

17

the forefinger of his right hand he wrote the sign of the cross upon the boy's forehead with the last drops of the wine.

The boy did not flinch, he trembled a little, that was all. Mr. Fortune bent down and welcomed him with a kiss.

He had waited, but after all not for long. The years in the bank, the years at St. Fabien, they did not seem long now, the time of waiting was gone by, drowsy and half-forgotten like a nightwatch. A cloud in the heavens had been given him as a sign to come to Fanua, but here was a sign much nearer and more wonderful: his first convert, miraculously led to come and kneel beside him a little after the rising of the sun. His, and not his. For while he had thought to bring souls to God, God had been beforehand with His gift, had come before him into the meadow, and gathering the first daisy had given it to him.

For a long while he stood lost in thankfulness. At last he bade the kneeling boy get up.

"What is your name?" he said.

"Lueli," answered the boy.

"I have given you a new name, Lueli. I have called you Theodore, which means 'the gift of God.' "

Lueli smiled politely.

"Theodore," repeated Mr. Fortune impressively.

The boy smiled again, a little dubiously this time. Then, struck with a happy thought he told Mr. Fortune the name of the scarlet blossoms that stood on either side of the cross. His voice was soft and pleasant and he held his head on one side in his desire to please.

"Come, Theodore, will you help me to put these things away?"

Together they rinsed the cup and the dish in the spring, folded the linen cloth and put them with the cross and the vases back into the black tin box. The flowers Mr. Fortune gave to the boy, who with a rapid grace pulled others and wove two garlands, one of which he put round Mr. Fortune's neck and one round his own. Then discovering that the tin box served as a dusky sort of mirror he bent over it, and would have stayed coquetting like a girl with a new coral necklace had not Mr. Fortune called him into the hut.

In all Lueli's movements there was a swiftness and a pliancy as though not only his mind but his body also were intent on complaisance and docility. A monkey will show the same adaptability, deft and pleased with its deftness, but in a monkey's face there is always a sad self-seeking look, and their eyes are like pebbles unhappily come alive. A bird, or a squirrel, or a lizard whisking over a stone have a vivid infallible grace, but it is inherent, they are made so, and however much one may admire or envy them, they do not touch one into feeling grateful to them for being what they are. As Mr. Fortune watched Lueli folding up the priestly clothes, patting them smooth and laying them in their box, he felt as though he were watching some entirely new kind of being, too spontaneous to be human, too artless to be monkey, too sensitive to be bird or squirrel or lizard; and he wished that he had been more observant of creation, so that he could find out what it was that Lueli resembled. Only some women, happy in themselves and in their love, will show to a lover or husband this kind of special grace; but this Mr. Fortune, whose love affairs had been hasty and conventional, did not know.

While they were breakfasting together in the verandah the missionary had a good look at his convert.

Lueli was of the true Polynesian type,

slender-boned and long-limbed, with small idle hands and feet: broadminded persons with no colour prejudices might have described him as aristocratic-looking. This definition did not occur to Mr. Fortune, who had no dealings with aristocrats and was consequently unaware of any marked difference between them and other people; but he reflected with satisfaction that the boy looked very refined for one who had been so recently a heathen. His eyes were rather small and his nose was rather snub, but these details did not mar the general good effects of regular features and a neatly-shaped head. Though when he talked he pulled very charming faces, in repose his expression was slightly satirical. In colour he was an agreeable brown, almost exactly the colour of a nutmeg; his hair was thick but not bushy and he wore it gathered up into a tuft over either ear, in much the same manner as was fashionable at the French Court in the year 1671.

In spite of his convert's advantageous appearance and easy manners Mr. Fortune judged that he was not the child of anyone particularly rich or distinguished; for in these islands where the poorest are scrupulously clean and the richest may wear for sole adornment the sophisti-

cated elegance of freshly gathered flowers, social standing may yet be deduced from the
degree of tattooing. Lueli had greaves and
gaiters of a pattern of interlacing bamboo-
shoots, and in addition a bracelet round his left
wrist and on his right shoulder-blade an amusing
sprig. But this was all. And from the elegance
of the designs and their wilful disposition it
seemed as though he had been decorated for no
better reason than the artist's pleasure.

When Mr. Fortune came to make enquiries
he found that he had judged rightly. Lueli was
one of a large family, which is rare in these
islands. His mother was a fat, giggling creature,
without a care in the world; even among the
lighthearted people of Fanua she and her brood
were a bye-word for their harum-scarum ways.
Their dwelling was a big tumble-down hut in
which there was scarcely ever anyone at home
except a baby; and though they had no apparent
father or other means of sustenance that was no
obstacle to well-being in this fertile spot where
no one need go hungry who could shake fruit
off a tree or pull fish out of the water.

All of the family were popular; Lueli in
particular, for his beauty and amiability, was a

regular village pet. But, whether it be that an uncommon share of good looks like a strain of fairy blood, sets their owners apart, or whether beautiful people are in some way aware of the firebrand they carry with them and so are inclined to solitariness, Lueli, like other beauties, had for all his affability a tincture of aloofness in his character. Although he was a pet, it was not a pet dog he resembled, solicitous and dependent, but a pet cat, which will leap on to a knee to be fondled and then in a moment detach itself, impossible to constrain as a beam of moonlight playing bo-peep through a cloud. So when he deserted the village and attached himself to the new-comer no one was hurt or surprised, they took it for granted that he would go where he pleased.

This complaisance had slightly shocked Mr. Fortune, particularly as it fell in so convenient to his wishes. It was most desirable, indeed almost necessary, that his convert should live with him, at any rate for the present, in order to assure and perfect the work of conversion. Afterwards the finished product could be let loose again, a holy decoy, to lure others into salvation's net. But good men do not expect silver spoons to be slipped into their mouths. Easy fortune finds them unprepared and a trifle suspicious.

Mr. Fortune sought to inoculate his good luck by a scrupulous observance of formalities. He put on his black felt hat and went to pay a call on Lueli's mother. On the fourth visit he happened to find her at home. Taking off the hat and bowing he addressed her with a long speech in which he drew a careful distinction between obedience to God and obedience to lawful authority. Lueli, said he, having become a Christian any attempts on her part to discourage him would be tempting Lueli to disobey God, therefore as God's priest it would be his duty to oppose them. On the other hand as Lueli's only visible parent and lawful guardian she had an absolute right to decide whether Lueli should remain at home, and if she wished him (Lueli) to do so, far from opposing her, he (Mr. Fortune) would enforce her authority with his own and insist upon the boy's return.

Lueli's mother looked rather baffled, and crumpled her face exactly as Lueli crumpled his in the effort to follow Mr. Fortune's explanation. But when he had finished she brightened, said that it was all a very good scheme, and asked if Mr. Fortune would like a netful of shrimps.

He spoke a little longer of his affection for the boy, and his plans for teaching him, explaining that though perhaps an European education might not be much use in Fanua, wherefore he was not proposing to trouble him with much arithmetic, yet a Christian education is useful anywhere and so Lueli must soon learn the Catechism; and then carrying the shrimps he set off to visit Ori.

Ori was the chief man of the island and it would be only civil and politic to consult him. Besides, there was always the chance that Ori might put a spoke in his wheel, a chance not to be missed by any conscientious Englishman. But when Ori had listened to the speech about obedience to God and obedience to lawful authority which Mr. Fortune delivered all over again (with of course suitable omissions and alterations) he also said that it was all a very good scheme. Wouldn't Mr. Fortune like a girl too?

Mr. Fortune refused, as politely as his horror would allow; for he had had more than enough of the girls of Fanua. He wished them no harm, it was his hope to live in charity with all men, girls included, and he had no doubt that when

25

they were converted they would become as much better as they should be. But in their present state they were almost beyond bearing. Once upon a time when he was still a bank clerk and had leisure for literature the phrase "a bevy of young girls" had sounded in his ears quite pleasantly, suggesting something soft as "a covey of partridges" but lighter in colour. Now it sounded like a cross between "a pack of wolves," "a swarm of mosquitoes," and "a horde of Tartars."

The girls of Fanua always went about in bevies, and ever since his arrival they had pestered him with their attentions. He had but to put his nose into the village for a score of brown minxes to gather round him, entangling him in garlands and snatching at his hat. If he walked on the beach at sunset repeating to himself that sonnet of Wordsworth's:

"It is a beauteous evening, calm and free,
The holy time is quiet as a Nun
Breathless with adoration; the broad sun
Is sinking down in its tranquillity;
The gentleness of Heaven is on the sea"

long before he had got to: "Dear child, dear girl that walkest with me here" he was sure to

be interrupted by sounds of laughter and splashing, and to find himself encompassed by yet
another bevy, naked from the sea, and begging
and cajoling him to go bathing with them.

If he fled to the woods they followed him,
creeping softly in his tracks. When he thought
himself safe and sat down to rest, a head and
shoulders would be thrust through the greenery;
soon there would be half a dozen of them
watching him, commenting and surmising on
his person, and egging each other on to approach nearer. If he got up to walk away they
burst out after him and taking hands entrapped
him in the centre of a dance, wanton enough
to inflame a maypole.

Once these nymphs surprised him bathing.
Fortunately the pool he was in was only large
enough to hold one at a time, so while it continued to hold him he was tolerably safe. But
it was tiresome to have them sitting all around
gazing at him as though he might shortly turn
into a satyr. He told them to go away, he even
begged them to do so, for the water was cold
and as modesty compelled him to sit with as
much of his person in the water as possible he
was growing cramped. But all was in vain; they
sat there as expectant as a congregation, and for

once sat in silence. His zeal told him that, tiresome as it all was, this opportunity for proselytiz-
ing should not be missed. Accordingly he began
to preach to them with chattering teeth, only his
shoulders appearing above the surface of the
water, draped in a sort of ruff or boa of water-
weed. He preached for an hour and twenty minutes, and then, seeing that they would neither
be converted nor go, he reared up out of the
pool, strode over the shoulder of the nearest
girl and proceeded (the word is more dignified
than walked), blue and indignant, toward his
clothes. Thank Heaven the young whores had
not noticed them!

The best thing that could be said for the girls
of Fanua, (unless judged as trials of temper,
mortifications, and potential stumbling-blocks,
in which case they would have received very
high marks) was that they afforded an admirable foil to Lueli's maidenly demeanour. Day
by day he unrolled such a display of the Christian virtues, was so gentle, so biddable, so deft to
oblige, so willing to learn, and just sufficiently
stupid to be no trouble, that Mr. Fortune felt he
could have endured even twice as many girls as
the price of being soothed by one such boy. He
had never beheld, he had never dreamed of such

a conversion. Indeed if it had been his own work he would have been uneasy, wondering if it were not too good to be true. But he acknowledged it to be the Lord's doing and so he was prepared for anything.

But he was not prepared for his paragon to disappear without a word of warning and stay away for three days and four nights. For the first twenty-four hours he thought little or nothing of it: Lueli was gone birding or gone fishing: he was playing with his friends in the village, or he might be on a visit to his mother. Mr. Fortune had no objection. On the contrary, he was rather pleased that the convert should thus hie him back to the company of his old acquaintance. There had been something disquieting almost, in the calm way Lueli had given his former life the go-by. He would not like to think him lacking in natural affection. So he slept through the first night and dabbled through the first day without feeling any uneasiness; but on the second night he dreamed that Lueli had come back, and waking from his dream he ran out into the dell to see if it were a true one.

There was no one there. He called: at first loudly, then he thought that Lueli might be hiding in the bushes afraid to come out lest he should be angry, so he called softly. Then he sat down in the verandah, for he knew there would be no more sleep for him that night, and began to worry, imagining all the dreadful things that might have befallen the boy, and reproaching himself bitterly for having allowed so much time to slip by before he awoke to the possibility of danger. Perhaps Lueli had been drowned. Mr. Fortune knew that he could swim like a fish, but he thought of drowning none the less. Perhaps running through the woods he had been caught like Absalom, or perhaps he had broken his leg and now, tired of calling for help, was lying snuffling with his face to the wet ground. Perhaps he had been carried off in a canoe by natives from some other island to serve as a slave or even as a meal.

"This is nonsense," said Mr. Fortune. "The boy is probably somewhere in the village. I will go down as soon as it is day, and enquire for him. Only when I know for certain that he is not there will I allow myself to worry."

For all that he continued to sit on the verandah, shredding his mind into surmises and waiting for the colour of day to come back to the whispering bushes and the black mountain. "In a little while," he thought, "the moon will be in her first quarter and Lueli will not be able to see his way back if he comes by night."

As soon as he decently could (for he had his dignity as a missionary to keep up) he walked to the village and made enquiries. No one had seen Lueli; and what was worse, no one could be persuaded into making any suggestions as to his whereabouts or being in the least helpful. There was some sort of feast toward: people were hurrying from house to house with baskets and packages, and the air was thick with taboos. Mr. Fortune hung about for a while, but no one encouraged him to hang on them. Presently he returned to the hut, feeling that the Fanuans were all very heathen and hateful.

Anxious and exasperated he spent the greater part of the day roaming about the woods, harking back every hour or so to the dell and the bathing pool on the chance that Lueli might have re-appeared. In the dell the shadows moved round from west to east and the tide brimmed and retrenched the pool; everything seemed to be in a conspiracy to go on as usual. By sunset he had tormented himself out of all self-control. His distress alternated with gusts

31

of furious anger against his convert. Blow hot, blow cold, each contrary blast fanned his burning. At one moment he pictured Lueli struggling in the hands of marauding cannibals: in the next he was ready to cast him off (that is if he came back) as a runagate, and began to prepare the scathing and renouncing remarks which should dismiss him. "Not that I am angry," he assured himself. "I am not in the least angry. I am perfectly cool. But I see clearly that this is the end. I have been deceived in him, that is all. Of course I am sorry. And I shall miss him. He had pretty ways. He seemed so full of promise."

And instantly he was ravaged with pity for the best and most ill-prized convert the world had ever seen; and now, perhaps, the world saw him no longer. Even if he had run away and was still frolicking about at his own sweet will, there was every excuse to be made for him. He was young, he was ignorant, he had not a notion how much suffering this little escapade entailed on his pastor, he belonged to a people to whom liberty is the most natural thing in the world. And anyhow, had he not a perfect right to run away if he chose to? "Good Heavens, do I want him tethered to me by a string?" So his passions whisked him round again, and he was angrier than ever with Lueli because he was also angry with himself for being ridden by what was little better than an infatuation, unworthy of a man and far more unworthy of a missionary, whose calling it is to love all God's children equally, be they legitimated or no. And he remembered uneasily how in visiting the village that morning he had not breathed a word of conversion.

The idea of having to worry about his own conduct as well as Lueli's agitated him so extremely that he fell on his knees and took refuge in prayer, imploring that his deficiencies might be overlooked and that his sins might not be visited upon Lueli; for it was no fault of the child's, he began to point out to the All-Knowing, that his pastor had chosen to erect him into a stumbling-block. But he was in too much of an upset to pray with any satisfaction, and finding that he was only case-making like a hired barrister he opened his prayer-book and set himself to read the Forms of Prayer to be Used by Those at Sea, for these seemed appropriate to his case. Thence he read on through the Form and Manner of Making, Ordaining, and Consecrating of Bishops, Priests, and Dea-

cons, and had persevered into the Accession
Service when there was a noise behind him. He
leapt up to welcome the truant. But it was only
a stray pig, looking curiously in on him from
the doorway.

"O pig!" Mr. Fortune exclaimed, ready just
then to disburden himself to anybody. But the
emotion betrayed in his hurt voice was so over-
whelming that the pig turned tail and bolted.

He addressed himself once more to the
Accession Service. The prayer-book lay face-
downward, something had fallen out of it, and
lay face-downward too. It was a little old-
fashioned picture with a lace-paper frame, one
of those holy valentines that lurk in pious
prayer-books, and in course of time grow very
foxed. He looked at it. It was a print of the
Good Shepherd, who with His crook was helping
a lost sheep out of a pit. Careless of His own
equilibrium, the Good Shepherd leant over the
verge of the rocks, trying to get a firm grip on
the sheep's neck and so haul him up into safety.

Smitten to the heart and feeling extremely
small, Mr. Fortune closed up the print in the
prayer-book. He had a shrewd suspicion that
this incident was intended as a slightly sarcastic
comment on his inadequacies as a shepherd. But

34

he took comfort too, for he felt that God had looked on his distress, even though it were with a frown. And all night (for he lay awake till dawn) he held on to this thought and endeavoured to wait still.

Having been so tossed up and down, by the morrow he was incapable of feeling anything much. He spent the day in a kind of stoical industry, visiting the islanders and preaching to them, though they heard him with even less acceptance than usual, for they were all engaged in sleeping off the feast. During the afternoon he washed his clothes and cleaned the hut and in the evening he practised the harmonium till his back smouldered with fatigue; and all night he lay in a heavy uncomfortable sleep, as though he were cased up in an ill-fitting leaden armour.

He awoke stupefied to bright daylight. He could scarcely remember where he was, or who he was, and his perplexity was increased by finding a number of presences, cold, sleek, and curved, disposed about his limbs. Serpents! In a panic that was half nightmare he sat up. His bed was full of bananas, neatly arranged to encircle him as sausages are arranged to encircle a Christmas turkey. Who had put bananas in his bed? Could it be——? He went swiftly and

35

silently to the door and peered into the dell. There by the spring sat Lueli, arranging shells round the water's edge as though he were laying out a garden. His back was turned, he was so absorbed in his game that he did not discover that he was being watched. Presently he rolled over and lay on his stomach, gently kicking his heels in the air.

Mr. Fortune had a good stare at him. Then he tiptoed back again and began to dress.

As a rule, Mr. Fortune was rather careless about his appearance, and compared to the islanders he was decidedly dirty, for whereas they would bathe themselves three times a day or more he considered that once was enough. But now he made his toilet with extraordinary circumspection and deliberation. He shaved himself as minutely as though he were about to attend an archidiaconal meeting, he parted his hair, he fastened every button with a twitch, he pulled his coat forward so that it should sit well on his shoulders, he wound up his watch and knotted his bootlaces so that they should not come undone. He even put on a hat.

All the while he had a curious sensation that he was dressing a man of stone that must needs be dressed like a dummy for of itself it was

36

senseless and immovable. Yet *he* was the man of stone, his fingers that slowly and firmly pushed the buttons through the button-holes and knotted the bootlaces were so remorselessly and stonily strong that if he had not been managing them with such care they would have ground the buttons to powder: and if he had allowed them for one moment to tremble the bootlaces would have snapped off in his grasp like black cotton threads.

Walking terribly and softly, and still in this curious stony dream, he stepped into the dell and advanced on Lueli. Lueli turned round. It seemed to Mr. Fortune that he was looking frightened but he could not be sure of this for his eyes also were partaking of the nature of stone, they did not see very clearly. He came up to Lueli and took hold of him by the shoulder and jerked him on to his feet.

Then, still holding fast to Lueli's shoulder he said:

"Where have you been?"

Lueli said: "I have been fishing with my two cousins. For three days we went in our boats and at night we sang."

But Mr. Fortune did not seem to have heard him, and said again:

"Where have you been?"

Lueli said: "We paddled round this island and away to the north-west to an islet of shells. I have brought you back these—look!—as a present."

For the third time Mr. Fortune asked:

"Where have you been?"

But this time he did not wait for an answer. Putting his face close to Lueli's and speaking with his eyes shut and in a low secret voice he began to scold him.

"Don't tell me where you've been. I don't care. Why should I care where you go? You made off without asking my leave, so what is it to me where you go to or how long you stay away? Nothing! For I cannot allow myself to love a boy who flouts me. While you were good I loved you, but that goodness didn't last long and I don't suppose it meant much. Why did you run away? If you had told me, if you had asked my leave I would have given it gladly. But of course you didn't, you went off without a word, and left me to worry myself half out of my mind. Not that I worried for long. I soon saw that you didn't care a snap of your fingers for me. If you were sorry I would forgive you, but you are not sorry, you are only

38

frightened. I am very angry with you, Lueli,
—for I cannot call you Theodore now."

Mr. Fortune's eyes were shut but he knew
that Lueli was frightened for he could feel
him trembling. After a minute he began again.

"I can feel how you tremble, but that is silly
of you, it only shows how little you understand
me. You have no reason to be frightened, don't
think I would punish you with blows for I
would never do such a thing, I don't approve
of it. But something I must do. I must tell you
when you do wrong, for it seems that you yourself don't know the difference between good
and bad. Why did you run away without telling
me where you were going? Was that like a
Christian? Was that like a child of God? Do
you suppose Samuel would have behaved so,
whom you pretend to take such an interest in?"

Mr. Fortune had almost talked himself out.
He was feeling dazed by the sound of his own
voice, sounding so different too, and he wished
Lueli would take a turn. But Lueli continued
to tremble in silence, he did not even wriggle,
so Mr. Fortune exerted himself to say a few
last words.

"Come now, Lueli, what is it to be? Don't
be frightened of me. I mean you nothing but

good. Perhaps I spoke too angrily; if so, you must forgive me. I was wrong to scold; but you really are maddening, and I have been very anxious about you and not slept much since you ran away. Anxiety always makes people seem stern."

Now he spoke almost pleadingly, but he still had his hand fast on Lueli's shoulder. At length he noticed this, for his hand was no longer stone but flesh and blood which ached from the intensity of its grip. He withdrew it, and in an instant Lueli had ducked sideways and with a spring like a frightened deer he fled into the bushes.

Mr. Fortune was in a state to do anything that was desperate, though what, he had not the slightest idea. But suddenly, and completely to his surprise, he found himself convulsed with laughter. He did not know what he was laughing at till in a flash he remembered Lueli's bolt for safety, and the ludicrous expression, half abject, half triumphantly cunning, with which he had made off. To run away again when he was in such disgrace for running away—this stroke, so utterly unexpected, so perfectly natural, rapt him into an ecstasy of appreciation. He forgave everything that had gone before for

40

leading up to this. And the brat had done it so perfectly, too. If he had practised nothing else for years he could not have surpassed that adroit, terror-stricken bound, nor the glance he cast over his shoulder—deprecating, defiant, derisive, alive.

He had never been so real before.

Mr. Fortune propped himself against a tree and laughed himself weak. He had laughed his hat off, his ribs ached, and he squealed as he fetched his breath. At last he could laugh no more. He slid to the ground and lay staring up into the branches with a happy and unseeing interest. He was looking at his thoughts: thoughts that at a less fortunate juncture might have pained him but that now seemed as remote and impersonal a subject for consideration as the sway and lapse of the fronds moving overhead.

How near he had gone to making an irremediable fool of himself, and perhaps worse than a fool! This came of letting oneself get into a fuss, of conscientiously supposing oneself to be the centre of the universe. A man turned into stone by a fury of self-justification, he had laid hold of Lueli and threatened him with pious wrath whilst all the time his longing had been to thrash the boy or to smite his body down on the grass and ravish it. Murder or lust, it had seemed that only by one or the other could he avenge his wounded pride, the priestly rage again the relapsed heretic. And then by the grace of God Lueli had leapt aside with that ludicrous expression, that fantastic agility: and by a moment's vivid realization of his convert's personality, of Lueli no longer a convert but a person, individual, unexpected, separate, he was released, and laughed the man of stone away.

He looked back on it without embarrassment or any feelings of remorse. Remorse was beside the point for what was so absolutely over and done with. Lueli had nothing to fear from him now—unless it were indigestion; for he proposed to make him some coco-nut buns as a peace-offering. They were quite easy to make. One just grated the coco-nut into a bowl, added a little water and drove the contents round with a spoon till they mixed. Then one formed the mixture into rocks, made each rock into a package with leaves, and baked them under the ashes. The results were quite palatable while they remained hot. And Lueli would take it as a compliment.

He would set about it presently. Meanwhile

he would lie here, looking up at the tree and taking an interest in his sensations. "I suppose it is partly reaction," he thought, "but I do feel most extraordinarily happy. And as mild as milk—as mothers' milk." He was not only happy, he was profoundly satisfied and rather pleased with himself, with his new self, that is.

"And why shouldn't I be? It is a great improvement on the old. It would be absurd to pretend now that I am not entirely different from what I was then. I might as well refuse to feel pleased at waking from a nightmare. A nightmare, a storm of error. The heavens after a thunderstorm, and the air, are so radiant, so fresh, that they seem to be newly-created. But they are not: the heavens and the eternal air were created once for all, it is only in man, that creature of a day, so ignorant and fugitive, that these changes can be wrought. The great thing, though, is not to make too much fuss about it. One should take things as they come, and keep reasonably busy. Those buns . . . How I must have frightened that pig!"

This time there were no bananas round him when he woke and no sign of Lueli. He did not fret himself: knowing how very unfrightening he was, he could not seriously apprehend that his convert was much frightened of him.

Nor was he. For hearing his name called he came out from where he had been reconnoitring in the bushes with scufflings so soft and yet so persistent that they might have been self-commendatory, serene, perfectly at his ease, with a pleasant smile and his head only slightly to one side. He showed no tactless anxiety to sound himself in Mr. Fortune's good graces. Only when Mr. Fortune ventured on a few words of apology did he seem at a loss, frowning a little, and wriggling his toes. He made no answer, and presently introduced a new topic. But he made it quite sufficiently clear that he would prefer an act of oblivion.

From that day the two friends lived together in the greatest amity. True, the very next week Lueli disappeared again. But this time Mr. Fortune remembered his psalm and waited with the utmost peacefulness and contentment. Indeed he found himself quite pleased to be left to the enjoyment of his own society. It had never seemed very enjoyable in old days but it was now. For on this enchanting island where everything was so gay, novel and forthcoming his transplanted soul had struck root enough to be responding to the favouring soil and sending up blossoms well worth inspection.

Beyond a few romantic fancies about bathing by moonlight and a great many good resolutions to keep regular hours, Mr. Fortune had scarcely propounded to himself how he would be suited by the life of the only white man on the island of Fanua. In the stress of preparation there had been no incitement to picture himself at leisure. It seemed that between converting the islanders and dissolving soup-squares he would scarcely have an unoccupied minute. Now he found himself in possession of a great many—hours, whole days sometimes, without any particular obligation, stretching out around him waste and tranquil as the outstretched blue sky and sparkling waves.

Leisure can be a lonely thing: and the sense of loneliness is terrifically enhanced by unfamiliar surroundings. Some men in Mr. Fortune's position might have been driven mad; and their madness would have been all the more deep and irrevocable because the conditions that nursed it were so paradisal. A delightful climate; a fruitful soil; scenery of extreme and fairy-tale beauty; agreeable meals to be had at the minimum of trouble; no venomous reptiles and even the mosquitoes not really troublesome; friendly natives and the most romantic lotus—these, and the prospect of always these would have mocked them into a melancholy frenzy.

But Mr. Fortune happened to be peculiarly well fitted to live on the island of Fanua. Till now there had been no leisure in his life, there had only been holidays; and without being aware of it, in body and soul he was all clenched up with fatigue, so that it was an intuitive ecstasy to relax. He could not have put a name to the strange new pleasure which was come into his existence. He supposed it was something in the air.

As it was with leisure, so it was with luxuriance. Most Englishmen who visit the South Sea Islands are in the depths of their hearts a little shocked at the vegetation. Such fecundity, such a largesse and explosion of life, trees waving with ferns, dripping with creepers, and as it were flaunting their vicious and exquisite parasites, fruits like an emperor's baubles, flowers triumphantly gaudy or tricked out with the most sophisticated improbabilities of form and patterning, all this profusion unbridled and untoiled for and running to waste disturbs them.

46

They look on it as on some conflagration and feel that they ought to turn the hose on it. Mr. Fortune was untroubled by any such thoughts, because he was humble. The reckless expenditure of God's glory did not strike him as reckless, and his admiration of the bonfire was never overcast by a feeling that he ought to do something about it. Indeed the man who ten years ago had been putting down in Mr. Beaumont's pass-book: Orchid Growers Ltd., £72 15s. 0d. had presently ceased to pay any special attention to the vegetables of Fanua, and was walking about among them as though they were the most natural thing in the world; which if one comes to reflect on it, in that part of the world they were.

But though he came to disregard the island vegetation he never ceased to be attentive to the heavens. To have time to watch a cloud was perhaps the thing he was most grateful for among all his leisurely joys. About a mile or so from the hut was a small grassy promontory, and here he would lie for hours on end, observing the skies. Sometimes he chose out one particular cloud and followed it through all its changes, watching how almost imperceptibly it amassed and reared up its great rounded cauliflower curves, and how when it seemed most proud and sculptural it began to dissolve and pour itself into new moulds, changing and changing, so that he scarcely had time to grasp one transformation before another followed it. On some days the clouds scarcely moved at all, but remained poised like vast swans floating asleep with their heads tucked under their wings. They rested on the air, and when they brightened, or changed their white plumage to the shadowy pallor of swans at dusk, it was because of the sun's slow movement, not their own. But those days came seldom, for as a rule the sea-wind blew, buoying them onward.

Lying on his stomach Mr. Fortune would watch a cloud come up from the horizon, and as it approached he would feel almost afraid at the silent oncoming of this enormous and towering being, an advance silent as the advance of its vast shadow on the sea. The shadow touched him, it had set foot on the island. And turning on his back he looked up into the cloud, and glancing inland saw how the shadow was already climbing the mountain side.

Though they were silent he imagined then a voice, an enormous soft murmur, sinking and swelling as they tumbled and dissolved and amassed. And when he went home he noted in his diary the direction of the wind and any peculiarities of weather that he had noticed. At these times he often wished, and deeply, that he had a barometer: but he had never been able to afford himself one, and naturally the people of the Mission had thought of a teapot.

On the first really wet day, however, he rushed out with joy and contrived a rain-gauge. And having settled this in and buttered its paws, he went for a long rejoicing walk, a walk full of the most complicated animal ecstasy, or perhaps vegetable would be the truer word; for all round him he heard the noise of the woods guzzling rain, and he felt a violent sympathy with all the greenery that seemed to be wearing the deepened colour of intense gratification, and with the rich earth trodden by the rain, and sending up a steam of mist as though in acknowledgment. And all the time as he trudged along he was pretending to himself how hardy he was to be out in such disagreeable weather, and looking forward to how nice it would be to get back to the hut and change into dry clothes, and boil a kettle for tea.

He was behaving as though he had never been out in the rain before. It had rained quite often in St. Fabien, indeed there were times when it seemed never to do anything else. But rain there had been a very different matter, veiling the melancholy quayside, clanking on the roofs of the rabble of tin church premises, and churning the soft grit of the roads into mud. It had rained in St. Fabien and he had constantly been out in it, but with no more ecstasy than he had known when it rained in Hornsey. No doubt the ownership of a rain-gauge accounted for much; but there was more to it than that—a secret core of delight, a sense of truancy, of freedom, because now for the first time in his life he was walking in the rain entirely of his own accord, and not because it was his duty, or what public opinion conceived to be so.

Public opinion was waiting for him in the hut when he got back. While he was still shaking himself like a dog in the verandah, Lueli appeared in the doorway, looking very dry and demure, and began to pet and expostulate in the same breath.

"How very wet! How very silly! Come in at once! Why do you go out when it rains?"

"It is healthy to go for a walk in the rain,"

replied Mr. Fortune, trampling firmly on public opinion.

"It would be better to stay under a roof and
sleep."

"Not at all. In England it rains for days at
a time, but everyone goes out just the same. We
should think it very effeminate to stop indoors
and sleep."

"I haven't been asleep the whole time," Lueli
remarked in a defensive voice. "That new
pot of yours—I've been out to fetch it in case it
got spoilt."

While he was drinking his tea, (Lueli drank
tea also, because his affection and pride made
him in everything a copycat, but he sipped it
with a dubious and wary expression), Mr. Fortune found himself thinking of England. He
thought about his father, a sanguine man who
suddenly upped and shot himself through the
head; and thence his thoughts jumped to a
Whitsuntide bank holiday, which he had spent
in a field near Ruislip. The sky was a pale
milky blue, the field was edged with some
dowdy elms and beyond them was a view of
distant gasworks. At two o'clock he had eaten
his lunch—a cold pork chop; and clear as ever

51

he could recall the exquisite unmeaning felicity of that moment.

How little pleasure his youth had known, that this outing should remain with him like an engraved gem! And now he scarcely knew himself for happiness. The former things were passed away—the bank with its façade trimmed with slabs of rusticated stone—a sort of mural tripe; his bed-sitting-room at "Marmion," 239 Lyttleton Road, N. E., so encumbered and sub-fusk, and the horrible disappointment of St. Fabien. There had passed the worst days of his life; for he had expected something of them, he had gone there with an intention of happiness and doing good. But though he had tried his best he had not been able to love the converts, they were degenerate, sickly, and servile; and in his discouragement he had thought to himself: "It's a good thing I know about book-keeping, for I shall never be fit to do anything better." And now he was at Fanua, and at his side squatted Lueli, carving a pattern on the rain-gauge.

The next day it rained again, and he went for another walk, a walk not so ecstatic as the former, but quite as wet and no doubt quite as healthy. Hollow peals of thunder rumbled through the cold glades, the chilling South wind blew and the coco-nuts fell thumping from the trees. He walked to his promontory and stood for some time watching the clouds—which were to-day rounded, dark and voluminous, a presentation to the eye of what the thunder was to the ear—and the waves. He felt no love for the sea, but he respected it. That evening the rain-gauge recorded 1.24.

The project of bathing by moonlight never came to much, for somehow when the time came he was always too sleepy to be bothered; but he was extremely successful in keeping regular hours, for all that so many of them were hours of idleness. Morning prayers, of course, began the day, and after prayers came breakfast. A good breakfast is the foundation of a good day. Mr. Fortune supposed that a great deal of the islanders' lack of steadfastness might be attributed to their ignorance of this maxim. Lueli, for instance, was perfectly content to have no breakfast at all, or satisfied himself with a flibberty-gibberty meal of fruit eaten off the bushes. Mr. Fortune made tea, softened and sweetened at once by coco-milk, and on Sundays, coffee. With this he had three boiled eggs. The eggs were those of the wild pigeon, eggs so small that three was really a quite moderate allowance. Unfortunately there was no certainty of them being new-laid, and very often they were not. So it was a notable day when it occurred to him that a native dish of bread-fruit sopped into a paste was sufficiently stodgy and sticky to be perfectly well eaten in lieu of porridge.

After breakfast and a pipe shared with Lūeli —he did not really approve of boys of Lueli's years smoking, but he knew that pipe-sharing was such an established Polynesian civility that Lueli's feelings would be seriously wounded if he didn't fall in with the custom—the hut was tidied, the mats shaken in the sun, and the breakfast things put away. Then came instruction in befitting branches of Christian lore: then, because the pupil was at hand, and it was well to make sure of him while he had him. For all that there were a good many holidays given and taken. With such an admirable pupil one could afford oneself the pleasure of bestowing it.

Since the teachings had to be entirely conversational, Lueli learnt much that was various and seemingly irrelevant. Strange alleys branched off from the subject in hand, references and similes that strayed into the teacher's discourse as the most natural things in the world had to be explained and enlarged upon. In the middle of an account of Christ's entry into Jerusalem, Mr. Fortune would find himself obliged to break off and describe a donkey. This would lead naturally to the sands of Weston-super-Mare, and a short account of bathing machines; and that afternoon he would take his pupil down to the beach and show him how English children turned sand out of buckets, and built castles with a moat round them. Moats might lead to the Feudal system and the Wars of the Barons. Fighting Lueli understood very well, but other aspects of civilization needed a great deal of explaining; and Mr. Fortune nearly gave himself heat apoplexy by demonstrating in the course of one morning the technique of urging a golf ball out of a bunker and how English housewives crawl about on their hands and knees scrubbing the linoleum.

After dismissing Lueli from his lessons, Mr. Fortune generally strolled down to the village to enlarge the work of conversion. By now he had given up general preaching and exhortation —not that he thought it a bad way to go to work, on the contrary, he knew that it had been sanctioned by the best Apostolic usage; but preaching demands the concurrence of an audience, even though it be one of fishes or pigs; and since he was no longer a novelty, the islanders had become as slippery as the one, as artful and determined in dodging away as the other. He practiced instead the Socratic method of pouncing upon any solitary and defenceless person who happened to pass by. And like Socrates he would lead them aside into the shade and ask them questions.

Many charming conversations took place. But nothing ever came of them, and the fields so white for the harvest continued to ripple and rustle in the sun, eluding all his efforts to reap and bind them into sheaves and carry them into God's barn in time for the harvest-home.

He had now been on the island for nearly six months and every day he knew himself to have less attractive power. How he wished that he had thought of bringing some fireworks with him! Two or three rockets touched off, a green Bengal light or a Catherine wheel, he would have been sure of a congregation then. And there is no religious reason why fireworks should not be used as a means to conversion. Did not God lure the fainting Israelites by letting Himself off as a pillar of fire by night? He thought, though, that had he fireworks at his command, he would draw the line at that variety which is known as British Cannon. They are very effective, but they are dangerous; and he did not wish to frighten his flock.

From mid-day till about two or three in the afternoon, there was no possibility of converting anybody, for the islanders one and all went firmly to sleep. This was the time when Mr. Fortune went for his daily walk. After so much endeavour he would have been quite pleased to take a nap himself; but he knew the value of regular exercise and by taking it at this time of day he was safe from molestation by the bevies. He usually ate a good deal of fruit on these walks, because he had not yet accustomed himself to such a long stretch between breakfast and dinner. Indeed for some time after his arrival on the island he felt rather underfed. Dinner consisted of more bread-fruit, messes prepared by Lueli, fish sometimes, roots flavoured with sea-water. Lueli preferred his fish raw. Sometimes Mr. Fortune made soup or opened a tin of sardines.

Dinner was immediately followed by afternoon tea. Mr. Fortune would not forego that

comfortable meal, so they had it as a sort of
dessert. Then followed a long sub-afternoon,
spent in various ways of doing nothing in particular. Lueli always went bathing then. He had
no theories about it being dangerous to bathe on
the heels of a large meal, and after an interval
for digestion Mr. Fortune bathed too. Sometimes they paid visits, or received them. On
these occasions Mr. Fortune never spoke of religion. He produced his pocket magnifying glass
and showed them his pores. At other times they
went sailing or took a stroll.

These were all pleasant doings, but perhaps
the moment he enjoyed best was when, dusk
having fallen, he lit the lamp. He had a peculiar
affection for his lamp. It hung from the ridge
pole of the hut and he felt about it much as
Sappho felt about the evening star. It shone as
though with a kindness upon everything that
was dear to him: upon his books, and the harmonium; upon the bowls and dishes and woven
mats that were both dear in themselves as tokens
of the islanders' goodwill, and endeared by use;
upon the wakeful shine of the tea-pot and the
black tin box, and upon Lueli's sleepy head.
He would often walk out into the darkness for

the pleasure of seeing his hut lighted up within, the rays of warm light shining through the chinks in the latticed walls as though they were shining through a very large birds' nest. Overhead were the stars trembling with the intensity of their remote fires. The air was very sweet and the dark grass gentle underfoot as he walked round about his home.

He whistled to himself, softly, an air that Delilah sings in the oratorio of Samson—a rather foolish chirruping tune, in which Handel expressed his private opinion of soprano Delilahs: but he liked the words——

> "How charming is domestic ease,
> A thousand ways I'll strive to please:"

(after that they ceased to be appropriate).

A thousand, thousand ways he would strive to please until he had converted all the islanders. And planning new holy wiles for the morrow he re-entered the hut to eat a slight supper, and perhaps to darn a rent or replace a button, and then to write up his diary, to read prayers, and so to end another day.

Saturday and Saints' days were holidays, for himself and Lueli both. Lueli disported himself as he pleased, and Mr. Fortune watched clouds. On Sundays they performed the services appointed by the Church of England.

There was a week or two when he believed that he was in the way to make another convert. She was a very old woman, extremely ugly, not very agreeable and rather doting. But she seemed perfectly able to understand about eternal life, and showed great anxiety to lay hold on it. Mr. Fortune visited her daily and tried hard to teach her the love of God, and the Christian belief. But she seemed deaf to all topics save one—and her anxiety to lay hold became as the days went by positively grasping.

One day the wife of Teioa, a sensible woman whom Mr. Fortune had a great respect for, came in with some food for the invalid and overheard part of their colloquy.

"Live for ever," she remarked rather scornfully to the missionary as they left the house. "Why, isn't she old enough already? How much more does she want?" And though Mr. Fortune deplored her blindness, yet in this particular instance he admitted to himself that she had perceived clearly enough, and that his old woman was no sort of genuine convert, only very old and frightened and rapacious. None the less he

continued to visit her, and to do what he could
to comfort her. And often as he sat by her
bedside he thought what a mystery this business
of eternal life is and how strangely, though
almost all desire it, they differ in their concep-
tion of what it is they desire; some, like Shakes-
peare (and how many others unknown?) coolly
confident of an immortality

"Where breath most breathes, even in the
    mouths of men";

some like Buddha, hoping for an eternal life in
which their own shall be absolved and lost,
some, like this old woman, desiring an eternity
like an interminable piece of string which she
could clutch one end of and reel forever about
herself. "And how do I desire it?" he thought.
"I want to feel it on every side, more abun-
dantly. But I want to die first."

In the end he grew quite attached to the old
creature, and when she died, he was sorry. He
would have liked, as a mark of respect, to attend her funeral (he certainly did not feel
that he had any claim to conduct it himself).
But no one suggested that he should, and he
hesitated to suggest it, lest he should be offend-
ing against some taboo. So he went off by him-

self for a day in the woods and thought about
her, and said a prayer or two. And in the
evening he returned to Lueli. One convert at
any rate had been granted to him, and perhaps
it would be greedy to want more, especially
as that one was in every way so exemplary and
delightful.

The two friends—for such they were despite
more than sixty degrees of latitude and over
thirty years between them (and the latter is a
more insuperable barrier than an equator) lived
together in the greatest amity. Lueli had now
quite given up running away. He settled down
to Mr. Fortune's ways and curled himself up
amidst the new customs and regulations as
peacefully as though he has never known any
other manner of existence. Indeed Mr. Fortune
was sometimes obliged to pack him off to the
village to play with the other boys, thinking that
it would harm him never to be with company
of his own age.

Lueli was no anchorite, he enjoyed larking
about the island with his friends as much as any
boy should do, but what he loved beyond anything was novelty, and for this he worshipped
Mr. Fortune, whose every action might reveal
some new and august entertainment. The faces

62

he made in shaving, the patch of hair on his
chest, his ceremonious method of spitting out
pips into his hand, the way in which his bootlaces went round the little hooks, his watch,
his pockets and the things he kept in them—
Lueli might grow accustomed to these daily
delights, but he did not tire of them any more
than Wordsworth tired of the Lesser Celandine.
And there was more than this, and much more:
prayer, the harmonium, the sewing-machine, religious instruction and occasional examples of
European cookery. Prayer Lueli had taken to
from the start, but the harmonium required
more getting used to. At first when Mr. Fortune played to him he would sit as close as
possible to the instrument, quivering like a dog
and tilting up his chin with such an ecstaticized
and woebegone look that Mr. Fortune almost
expected him to howl; and thinking that he
didn't really enjoy it he would leave off playing.
But Lueli would then edge a little closer and
beg for more and Mr. Fortune was only too
glad to comply.

Like the harpsichord, the harmonium has a
repertory of its own, pieces that can only be
properly rendered on this instrument. Naturally
I do not speak of the harmonium compositions

63

of such recent composers as Schoenberg, or Max
Reger: these would have been too difficult for
Mr. Fortune to play even if they had been
stocked by the music-shop he had frequented. But
without being in any way a virtuoso—and some
think that the harmonium, being essentially a
domesticated instrument, sober and of a religious nature, is inherently unsuited for dis-
plays of skill—Mr. Fortune played quite nicely
and had a repertory of many classical larghettos
and loud marches, besides of course, the usual
hymns and chants. Haydn was his favourite
composer; and arrangements from the string
quartets go rather well on the harmonium.

Lueli too was a musician after a simpler
fashion. He had a wooden pipe, rather like a
flageolet, of a small compass and a sad squeaky
tone; and the two friends passed many happy
evenings entertaining each other with their performances. First Mr. Fortune obliged, leaning
forward at an acute angle on the music stool,
his knees rising and falling like parts of a machine, his face very close to the music, his large
hands manœuvring among the narrow keys, or
sometimes hovering like a bee in a flower-
border over the ranks of stops, pulling out one,
hitting another back with a tap, as though his

64

fingers could read, though rather short-sightedly, in black Gothic lettering on the ivory knobs such names as Gamba, Corno di Bassetto, Bourdon, or Dulciana. And then, when rising he released the last throbbing chord and stretched himself (for he was a tall man and in order to adjust his body and legs to the instrument he had to assume a rather cramped position) it was pleasant to see Lueli discoursing music in his turn, and a curious study in contrasts. For the boy sat cross-legged on the floor, or leant against the wall in the attitude of the boy in the statue, an attitude so physically nonchalant, so spiritually intent that whoever looks at the statue, or even a cast of it or a photograph, understands, sometimes with a kind of jealous horror, how musicians are free of a world of their own, inhabiting their bodies as it were nominally or by proxy—just as we say of a house: That is Mr. So and So's; but the house is empty save for a sleepy caretaker, the owner is away travelling in Africa.

Lueli's tunes were very long tunes, though the phrases composing them were short; the music seemed to waver to and fro, alighting unexpectedly and then taking another small flight, and listening to it was like watching a bird

65

flitting about in a bush; the music ends, the bird flies away; and one is equally at a loss to explain why the bird stayed so long and seemed so busy or why it suddenly made up its mind that the time had come for a longer flight, for a flight that dismisses it from our vision.

To tell the truth, Mr. Fortune was not as much impressed by Lueli's music as Lueli was by his. His chin even sank further into his chest as he sat, his listening flesh was unmoved and he never felt the least impulse to howl. Mr. Fortune, in spite of his superior accomplishments, his cultivated taste and enough grasp of musical theory to be able to transpose any hymn into its nearly related keys, was not so truly musical as Lueli. For instance, he never had the least idea whether Lueli's tunes were lively or sad. They all seemed alike to him. But Lueli learnt almost immediately to distinguish between a march and a sentimental piece, and as the harmonies grew more and more passionate his chin would lift higher, his mouth would contract, and the shadow of his long eyelashes would shorten up over his cheek.

It would have been pleasant if the two mūsicians could have joined forces. Mr. Fortune by listening very often and pretty intently to

Lueli's rambling tunes was able to memorize two of them, as he believed, perfectly. Sending Lueli down to the village he spent an afternoon practicing these two melodies on the harmonium and putting in a part for the left hand. It would make an agreeable surprise for his boy, he thought, to hear his tunes played by someone else; and then with Lueli playing his pipe while he supported the melody with chords and figurations they would achieve a duet. But the surprise fell quite flat; perhaps Mr. Fortune's European harmonies had queered the pitch, perhaps he had misunderstood the time-values, in any case, Lueli showed no signs of recognizing the tunes, and even when their identity was pointed out to him he seemed doubtful. As for the duet plan, it was not feasible, for the harmonium was tuned to the mean-tone temperament and Lueli's pipe obeyed some unscientific native scale; either alone sounded all right but in conjunction they were painfully discordant.

Finding it impossible to convert Lueli's pipe, Mr. Fortune next essayed to train his voice to Christian behaviour. In this he was more successful; Lueli's voice was of a nondescript newly-broken timbre. He couldn't always control it and Mr. Fortune had to smoke his pipe very hard in order not to laugh at the conjunction of Lueli's expression, so determined in well-doing, and the vagaries of his voice wandering from the straight path and ricochetting from note to note.

He also taught him to whistle, or tried to, for he was rather shocked at the idea of a boy not knowing how to whistle, explaining to him before hand the secular nature of the act, and forbidding him to whistle tunes that had any especially sacred associations. But though Lueli screwed up his lips and almost burst himself taking in breath his whistling remained of a very girlish incompetent kind. On the other hand he showed an immediate aptitude for the vulgar kind of whistling which is done with a blade of grass. The first hearing of this was one of the pleasantest surprises that his pastor gave him. He mastered the technique in a few minutes and raced off to show the new accomplishment to his friends in the village. The fashion caught on like wildfire, and soon every boy on the island was looking for the proper blades of grass which are called squeakers. The woods rang with their performances and the parrots looked down with awe and astonishment at hearing men producing sounds so much more ear-splitting than anything they could achieve themselves.

The fashion raged like wildfire and like wildfire burnt itself out. The groves were peaceful again, that is to say peaceful as any groves can be with parrots in them (not that the reader should suppose that the parrots at Fanua were like the parrots in the Zoological Gardens: oppression makes them much noisier); and every one was out in the salt-meadows, passionately flying kites.

The islanders were like that; enthusiastic and fickle, they would wear a whim to shreds and cast it away in the course of a week. Lueli was as bad, if it had not been for Mr. Fortune he would never have persevered in anything. It was provoking for a master to find his pupil so changeable and inconstant, all the more so because of Lueli's extraordinary docility and aptitude in learning. Nothing could have exceeded the readiness with which he accepted a new idea; and finding him so swift to become a Christian Mr. Fortune used to wonder why the other islanders would not respond as pleasantly to his teaching, for at this time he was still in hopes of converting the whole island. He preached to them, he prayed among them, every night and morning he prayed for them, he gave them biscuits and showed them pictures. They behaved themselves to him most charmingly, tactfully overlooking his blunders in etiquette, accepting him as their friend, though an unaccountable one. But his message they would not accept, it slid off them as though their very innocence and guilelessness had spread a fine impermeable film over their souls.

"After all," thought Mr. Fortune: "I have not made a single convert in this island though it is now almost a year since I came. For I did not convert Lueli, God gave him to me (by the way I must remember to call him Theodore). And God still withholds the others."

This was a comfortable point of view. It satisfied Mr. Fortune, all the more so since it agreed so aptly with his psalm, of which the last verse runs: "And that Thou, Lord, art merciful: for Thou rewardest every man according to his work." And he quoted this verse of it in the report which he handed to Archdeacon Mason on returning to St. Fabien to buy more stores and give an account of his ministry.

The Archdeacon frowned slightly when he laid down the report, which was a pretty piece of work, for Mr. Fortune had written it in his neatest hand and Lueli (under his direction) had tinted blue, fawn-colour and green the little sketch-map of the island which embellished it as a frontispiece.

The next day Mr. Fortune called upon his superior.

"My dear Fortune," said he after a few polite questions about the soil of Fanua and its marriage ceremonies, "this is excellent," (here he tapped the report which lay on the table). "Indeed I may say it is idyllic. But you must allow me to make one comment, you must let me tell you that there is such a thing as being too modest. Believe me, conversions at the rate of one *per annum* are not an adequate reward of your works. God's grace is infinite, and I am sure that your labours have been most truly conscientious; and yet you say you have only made one convert. This is not enough—mind, I would not speak a word of blame. I only say— if I may so express myself—that there must have been a leakage somewhere, a leakage!"

He paused. Mr. Fortune looked at his hands and realized how sunburnt they had become.

"Compel them to come in, you know."

Mr. Fortune wondered if he should confess to his superior the one so nearly disastrous occasion when he had tried to use compulsion. But the Archdeacon's metaphor about the leakage had pained him and he decided not to. Instead he asked the Archdeacon how he would advise him to act in order to convert the whole island.

It was rather a shock to him to be recommended to take a leaf out of the Jesuits' book. However on the first evening of his return to the island he began to make some discreet enquiries of Lueli about what gods the islanders worshipped, though being very careful to convey by his tone and choice of words that he thought it a terrible pity that they should not worship his.

"Oh, they," said Lueli, offering him some more fruit, which Mr. Fortune refused since he had been stuffed with gifts in kind ever since the moment he got out of the launch. "Oh, they—they only worship one god."

This answer did not sound quite as it should: and in deference to his recent memories of the Archdeacon Mr. Fortune ran his convert through the Apostle's Creed before proceeding with his enquiries. It was quite all right. Lueli remembered the creed without a single lapse, and on further questioning Mr. Fortune discovered that the islanders worshipped one god each, a much more suitable state of affairs for heathens; although on thinking it over before he fell asleep the missionary reflected that in the island of Fanua conversion must necessarily be a slow business since he would have to break the faggot stick by stick. Just before he lost consciousness he began to wonder what sort of god Lueli had worshipped.

In the morning he remembered his curiosity. He said to Lueli: "What god had you before I came and taught you to know the true God?"

"I'll show him to you," said Lueli; and running into the bushes he presently returned with an idol about two foot long.

Mr. Fortune looked at the idol very seriously, almost respectfuly, as though he were measuring swords with an adversary. It was a rather well-looking idol, made of wood and nicely polished, and he was pleased to note that it was not obscene; but for all that a slight shudder ran through his flesh, such as one feels on looking at a dead snake even though one knows that it is a dead one.

"Drop it," he commanded, and the boy laid it down on the grass between them. Mr. Fortune remembered the words of a female mis-

sionary from China who had visited St. Fabien
on a tour. "The first thing I make my converts
do," she had said, and as she spoke she clenched
her hands till the knuckles showed up as bones:
"is to destroy their idols. Then I can feel sure of
them. And not till then."

Talking over her lecture afterwards Mr. Fortune had been of the opinion of the majority:
that the lady missionary had been right. "I don't
agree at all," said his friend, Henry Merton.
"We teach that idols are the works of men's
hands, things of wood and stone. To insist on
their destruction is to show our converts that we
believe in them ourselves, that we look on them
with anxiety and attribute power to them. No,
no, it is silly to take any idol so seriously!" And
Mr. Fortune, who was humble before others,
thought that after all he had judged too hastily
and that his friend was in the right of it.

Soon after that, Henry Merton had died, and
the words of the dead have a special value. Mr.
Fortune remembered his friend's opinion, but
he also remembered the female missionary. She
had spoken with an air of authority, and for all
he knew she might be dead too, she might even
be a martyr. He stood and looked at Lueli's idol
which lay on the grass between them and he

74

wondered if he should tell Lueli to burn it. At last without saying anything he walked into the hut. When he came out again Lueli was scouring a wooden bowl and the idol was gone.

One of the Archdeacon's first questions about the convert of Fanua was: Had Mr. Fortune dressed him properly? And Mr. Fortune had replied with perfect candour that he had been too busy caring for his soul to think of his clothing. This too the Archdeacon had objected to, saying that dress made a great difference, and that when the other islanders saw Lueli dressed befittingly they would become aware of their nakedness and wish to be converted and wear white raiment.

"But they have seen me, *I* have never omitted to dress myself since I have lived at Fanua."

"No, no, of course not," answered the Archdeacon, a little testily, for really the missionary's simplicity was making him very argumentative and tiresome. "But that is not to the point, for you surely don't suppose that they look on you as one of themselves. You must clothe that boy, Fortune, you must make him wear trousers and a tunic. And at night he must wear a nightshirt."

So now, seeing that the idol was gone, Mr.

75

Fortune called Lueli into the hut and began to measure him. He had never learnt tailoring, however he supposed that by taking great care and doing his best he could turn out a suit of clothes which might insinuate the fact of their nakedness to the islanders of Fanua, even if it had no other merit. He measured Lueli, he wrote down the measurements, he made his calculations and drew a sort of ground plan. Then he fetched a roll of white cotton and having laid it upon the floor and tethered it with some books he crawled about on all fours cutting out the troūsers and the tunic with a pair of nail-scissors; for he thought that the nightshirt might rest in abeyance for the present.

The nail-scissors could only manage very small bites, and by the time the cutting-out was completed he was rather dizzy and very hot from taking so much exercise on his knees.

"That will do for the present," he thought, rolling up the pieces. "This afternoon I will visit my parishioners. Perhaps as they have not seen me for a week they will be more inclined to listen to my teaching. And I must keep my eyes open for idols."

But early on the morrow Mr. Fortune got out the sewing-machine and continued his ca-

reer as a tailor. The sewing-machine was suffering from the sea-air, it needed a great deal
of oil and adjustment before it could be got
to run smoothly, but he mastered it in the end
and began to sew up the seams. As time went on
he grew more and more excited. He worked the
treadles faster and faster, he had never, even
for the most spirited march, trodden the pedals
of his harmonium so frantically; the machine
rocked under his zeal and all the time the needle
kept darting up and down, piercing the cotton
with small accurate stabs in a way that seemed
to express a kind of mechanical malevolence.
The seams were all finished, the hems were
turned up; now it was evening, there was nothing left but the buttons. Those he must put on
by hand.

All day Lueli had sat beside him watching
his performance with rapture. It was the machine which ravished him, he was not so much
interested in the clothes. But when Mr. Fortune
called him in a rather solemn voice and began
to dress him, holding up the tunic above his
head as though it were a form of baptism, he
too began to put on looks of solemnity and
importance.

The tunic fitted tolerably enough though

there was no elegance about it; but alas! the trousers were a sad blow to Mr. Fortune. For he had designed them on a two-dimensional basis, cutting out the back and the front in one operation on a doubled fold of the cloth, and forgetting that even the slimmest boy is bulkier behind than in front; so that when attired in these unfortunate garments it was difficult for Lueli to move and almost impossible for him to sit down. He, in his innocence, thought the trousers all that they should be, and late as it was he wished to run down to the village in order to wake up his friends and show them his fine clothes. But Mr. Fortune bade him take them off. It made his heart bleed to see his boy made such a figure of fun, and when the living Lueli emerged from his white cotton sepulchre he privately called the Archdeacon a fool and foreswore the idea of the nightshirt for good and all. But on the next day and on the next again he struggled to make a practicable pair of trousers, and in the end he produced a pair that were rather on the baggy side perhaps, but still they were tolerable.

Unfortunately by this time his convert's ardour was somewhat quenched. He had been measured so often, he had stood still to be fitted

when he wanted to go fishing, he had had
pins run into him and all this had made this
particular novelty seem rather a tedious example of his pastor's odd ways. So though he
put on his white raiment at command and
walked decorously through the village beside
Mr. Fortune to be an object lesson, his demeanour while admirably meek and civil, wasn't
much of an advertisement for the happiness of
those who are clothed in the whole armour of
God.

The Archdeacon's theory was not borne out
by events. The islanders were too much struck
and roused to speculation by the sight of Lueli's
apparel to spare a thought for their own nakedness. At first they were of the opinion that this
was some new and powerful taboo invented by
the stranger. They shrank back, and averted
their eyes as if from some improper spectacle.
Lueli's mother was actually moved to a display
of maternal feeling. She rushed weeping from
the crowd, hurled herself at Mr. Fortune's knees
and began to implore him not to ruin the boy's
prospects. Disentangling himself a little pet-
tishly from her pleadings Mr. Fortune explained
that clothing such as this would do Lueli nothing but good: indeed, she herself would be none

79

the worse for something of the sort. She took
him at his word, before he could stay her she
had torn the clothes off her son and was squirm-
ing into them. She was several sizes too fat and
Mr. Fortune saw his seams being rent open in
all directions. He had to bribe her with a promise of the blue glass mulberries from his Christmas tree selection before she would consent to
undress. Finally he had to ease her out himself.
It was a good thing that the Archdeacon was
not present, but for all that Mr. Fortune half
wished that he had been.

On their return he sewed up the seams once
more and called Lueli. The boy began to protest
and argue. Then he changed his methods and
started coaxing. Mr. Fortune had his own ideas
as to how Lueli should be managed. Rising dis-
creetly he opened the harmonium and said that
it was time to study another hymn.

That night he lay awake, wondering what he
would do if his convert rebelled. He had already
decided to drop the Archdeacon's tactics at the
first seemly opportunity: but he wished to choose
the opportunity and do the dropping himself.
He might have spared himself this anxiety. On
the morrow Lueli donned the trousers and the
tunic with a very matter of course air, and half

an hour later went off to bathe. And it was a
sure thing that if formerly he had bathed
twice or thrice a day he now bathed as often
again, undressing with a bland smile and folding up his white raiment with the utmost neat-
ness. Of course it was a pretext; and the missionary wondered if his charge was learning
to be deceitful. But Lueli's deceitfulness was so
very open and unconcerned that it could scarcely
be reckoned as the genuine article.

The clothes were always deposited very carefully in some place where they would have
every opportunity of happening to fall into the
sea. At the end of a week they were so sat-
urated with brine as to be quite unwearable.
Exercising his authority Mr. Fortune forbade
Lueli to wear them any more.

Lueli would bathe anywhere; he seemed
equally happy lolling on the Pacific Ocean or
folded up in a pool the size of a bedroom basin
with a little waterfall splashing on his head. Mr.
Fortune was more ceremonious. It was he who
instituted the bathing pool as a regular adjunct
to their life.

About a half mile from the hut and near the
cloud observatory was a small rocky cove with
a half-moon of white shell-beach and a slope of

fine sward running back into the woods. A
small rivulet debouched here, very convenient
for washing off the sea-salt in; and as the mouth
of the cove was guarded by a barrier of coral-
reef the water within was almost as still as a
lake and so clear that one could look down and
see the weeds twenty feet below slowly twirl-
ing their vast brown or madder-coloured rib-
bons, and the fish darting among them.

Mr. Fortune often thought of Robinson
Crusoe and his man Friday as he sat on the
rocks watching Lueli at his interminable diver-
sions in the pool. Living on an island alone with
his convert, spiritually alone at any rate, for
though he had not given up hope of the other
Fanuans and still visited them pretty frequently
he could never feel the kinship with them which
he felt so securely with Lueli, the comparison
could scarcely fail to occur to him. And he
thought gratefully how much happier he was
than the other man. *He* was ideally contented
with his island and with his companion, he had
come there by his own wish and he liked the
life so well that he proposed to continue in it
until his death. So little did it distress him to be
away from civilization that he was of his own
will paring away the slender bonds that tied

him to the rest of the world. For after the first
visit to St. Fabien he had paid no more, and for
the last twelve-month he had not even bestirred
himself to write a report to be sent by canoe to
the island of Maikalua, where a local steamer
touched once a month. But poor Crusoe had no
such contented mind. His is a tragic story, albeit
considered so entertaining for school-boys: and
though his stay on the island taught him to find
religion it did not teach him to find happiness,
but whether at work or at leisure he was always
looking with a restless and haggard stare at the
rigid horizon, watching for a sail, enemy or
friend, he knew not.

"I see numbers of goats. Melancholy reflections." What a world of sombre and attentive
ennui, thought Mr. Fortune, is summed up in
those words! The goats might supply him with
suppers and raiment, but not with a cheerful
thought. Their antics were wasted on him, he
observed them without a smile, without sympathy, as unresponsive to natural history as the
traduced Alexander Selkirk of Cowper's poem;
for the real Alexander was a much more congenial character who sometimes danced and sang
with his troop of pet animals. True, Robinson
was fond of his dog, and kind to him, setting

him on his right hand at meal times even after he was grown "very old and crazy." He also gave a decent burial to the two cats. But these were English animals, fellow-countrymen, assuring relics of the time when he had been knolled to church with other Christians: and it was for this he cherished them, clinging to them with a trivial and desperate affection.

No! In spite of his adventurous disposition and his knowledge of the world, he was not really suited to life on an island, this man who is for all time the representative of island-dwellers. Of course, his island was very different from Fanua: larger, not so beautiful probably; certainly not so convenient. And no doubt the presence of natives would have made a great difference to him. He was the sort of man who would soon marry. "But to be honest with myself," thought Mr. Fortune, "though I came here to convert the islanders, except for my Friday I don't think I should miss their company if it were withdrawn. My happiness is of a rather selfish and dream-like kind and I take my life very much for granted. Why, I have not even walked round the island. That would seem strange to some, they would not believe in me. I should seem as absurd and idyllic as those other Robinsons, that Swiss family, who whenever they needed anything found it cast up on shore or growing on a tree. I should be even more unlikely than Leila."

And he began to ponder on how many years had gone by since he last thought of Leila. She came in a book belonging to his step-sister, and he had read it secretly and rather bashfully because it was a book for girls. But he had been obliged to read on for the subject of islands had always enthralled him. Leila was shipwrecked on a desert island with her papa, her nurse, a spaniel, and a needle. One day the needle was dropped by Leila and lost in the sand. Here was a sad to-do! But the nurse, a very superior politic woman, bade the spaniel Go seek; and presently he uttered a yelp and came running towards them with the needle sticking in his nose.

A very thin story! Yet it might have happened for all that it was so fortunate. Things do sometimes fall out as we would have them, though perhaps not often, for it is always the happy coincidences which are hardest to credit. Man, however gullible and full of high ideals for his own concerns, is suspicious of good-fortune in general. If Robinson had enjoyed himself on the island he would not have been received as somebody in real life.

"But I am in real life," thought Mr. Fortune, adroitly jerking a limpet to assure himself of being so, "although I am so happy in my lot. I am real too, as real as Robinson. Some people might even say I was more real than he, because my birth is mentioned in the church register, and I used to pay income-tax, whereas he was only entered at Stationers' Hall. But I don't agree with them. I may seem to have the advantage of him now, but it is only temporary. In twenty years' time, maybe less, who will even remember my name?"

From such reflections he would be diverted by Lueli politely handing him a long streamer of sea-weed, dripping and glistening, and freshly exhaling its deep-sea smell—a smell that excites in one strongly and mysteriously the sense of life—or beckoning to him with a brown hand that held a silver fish. These advances meant that Lueli thought it time for Mr. Fortune to bathe too, and to take his swimming-lesson—a turning of the tables which the convert considered extremely amusing and satisfactory. Mr. Fortune was a very

86

poor pupil. As a child he had never done more
than to paddle about, and now he was too old to
learn easily. He did not lack goodwill or per-
severance, but he lacked faith. Faith which can
remove mountains can also float. Mr. Fortune
had not enough of it to do either. In the depths
of his heart he mistrusted the sea, an ambiguous
element. The real sea beyond the reef he never
dreamed of venturing in, he could imagine how
the long nonchalant rollers would pick him up
and hurl him with their casual strength upon
the rocks. Even in this sheltered pool he could
gauge their force; for though scarcely a ripple
traversed the surface, to every leisurely surge
that crashed on the reef the pool responded
throughout its depth with a thrill, a tremor, an
impulsion, and the streamers of sea-weed turned
inland one after another as though they were
obeying a solemn dance music.

But for all his mistrust he enjoyed bathing,
indeed the mistrust put a tang into his enjoyment. And with looks of derring-do he struck
out into the middle of the pool, his teeth set,
his eyes rolling, splashing horribly and snorting
a good deal, labouring himself along with uncouth convulsions, while Lueli swam beside him

or round him or under him as easily as a fish
and with no more commotion, seeming like a
fish to propel himself and change his direction
with an occasional casual flip.

The further half of the pool, under the wall
of rocks whence Lueli used to dive, was extremely deep. Whenever he had got so far Mr.
Fortune was afraid and not afraid. He had a
natural fear but he had a reasonable trust; for
he knew that while Lueli was by he would never
drown. It was sweet to him to be thus relying
upon his convert—that was part of the pleasure of bathing. On shore it was fit and proper
that Lueli should look up to him and learn from
him; but every affectionate character even
though it be naturally a dominant one, spending
itself by rights in instruction and solicitude,
likes sometimes to feel dependent. People, the
most strong-minded people, perfectly accustomed to life, being ill may discover this; and as
they lie there, passive, tended and a little bewildered, may be stirred to the depths of their
being by finding themselves wrapped once more
in the security of being a good child. Mr. Fortune bathing in the pool did not go quite so far
as this. His dependence was not quite so emo-

tional and he was too busy keeping himself afloat to analyse his feelings very carefully; but he liked to depend on Lueli, just as he liked Lueli to depend on him.

Though so ready to learn swimming from Lueli he was less favourably inclined to another of his convert's desires: which was to oil him. He would not for the world have had Lueli guess it but at the first proposal of these kind offices he was decidedly shocked. Lueli oiled himself as a matter of course, and so did everybody on the island. They also oiled each other. Mr. Fortune had no objection. It was their way. But below all concessions to broadmindedness his views on oiling were positive and unshakable. They were inherent in the very marrow of his backbone, which was a British one. Oiling, and all that sort of thing, was effeminate, unbecoming, and probably vicious. It was also messy. And had Hector and Achilles, Brutus and Alexander detailed before him, all of them sleek and undeniably glistening as cricket-bats, he would have been of the same opinion still.

"No, thank you," he said, firmly putting aside the flask of scented coco-nut oil (scented, too!). Or: "Not just now, Lueli, I am going for a

walk. Exercise is the best thing after bathing."
Or again: "Unfortunately oil has a very pain-
ful effect on my skin."

But he knew all the time that sooner or later
he would have to muffle up his prejudices and
give in, for every day Lueli began to look, first
more hopeful and then more hurt, and was per-
petually (if figuratively) standing on his head
in the attempt to produce some unguent which
could not injure his friend's sensitive skin. So
when he sprained his knee jumping off a rock
he welcomed the pretext with feeings intri-
cately compounded of relief and apostasy. For
some weeks he confined the area of effeminacy
to his left knee, and on one occasion he was base
enough to lacerate the flesh in secret with a fish-
hook in an attempt to justify the statement
about his skin. But Lueli was so piteously full
of compunction and so certain that if he climbed
a yet higher tree or went in a canoe to another
island he would be able to procure a balm entirely blameless that Mr. Fortune was ashamed
of the prank and counterfeited no more. Indeed
he was beginning to enjoy what he assured himself was not oiling, nothing of the sort, but a
purely medicinal process. And by the time he
had finished with the sprain it struck him that

something of the same kind might be good for his rheumatism. After all there was nothing but what was manly and might quiet him in Elliman's Embrocation—used extensively by many athletes and as far as he could remember by horse-doctors.

Mr. Fortune kept his rheumatism up and down his back, but inevitably a little of the embrocation slopped over his shoulders. By the end of six months he was stretching himself out for Lueli's ministrations as methodically as when in the old days at the corner of the Hornsey Parade he offered one foot and then the other to the boot-black. It did him a great deal of good and improved his appearance tenfold, though that did not matter to him. Nothing could make him fat, but he began to look quite well-liking. The back of his hands grew smooth and suent, he ceased to have goose-flesh on his thighs, and one day, regarding himself more attentively than usual in the little shaving mirror, he discovered that somehow his expression had changed. How and why he would not stoop to examine into; but Lueli could have told him. For when he came to the island his face was so parched and wrinkled that it was like a mask of rough earthenware, and his eyes being the only surface in it that looked alive, also looked curiously vulnerable. But now his face had come alive too and instead of wrinkles had rather agreeable creases that yielded and deepened when he laughed. And his eyes were no longer vulnerable, but just kind.

But if Mr. Fortune had altered during his three years on the island, Lueli had altered a great deal more. Not in character though—he was still the same rather casual compendium of virtues and graces; nor in behaviour—for he still hung affectionately and admiringly round Mr. Fortune with a dependence which for all its compliance and intimacy yet remained somehow gaily and coolly aloof, so that the priest felt more and more that what he was rearing up was in truth a young plant, a vine or a morning glory, which while following all the contours of the tree it clings to draws from its own root alone a secret and mysterious life in which the very element of dependence is as secret and mysterious as the rest.

In the beginnings of an intimacy one seems to be finding out day by day more about another person's inner life and character. But after a certain stage has been reached not only does further exploration become impossible but things which one thought were discoveries become suddenly meaningless and irrevelant and one finds that one really knows nothing about them, nothing at all. They sit beside one, they turn their heads and make some remark, and the turn of the head and the tone of the voice and even what they say seem all familiar and already recognized in one's heart: but there can be no knowing why they turned and spoke at that moment and not at another nor why they said what they did and not something totally different. Though one might expect this realization to be agonizing it is so much part of the natural course of things that many people do not notice it at all and others, whilst acknowledging that something has happened, account for it perfectly to their own satisfaction by hypotheses which are entirely inapplicable.

Mr. Fortune, for instance, finding that he knew no more of Lueli than at the moment when he first beheld him kneeling on the grass, said to himself that he now knew him so well that he had grown used to him. In the same breath he was able to rejoice in a confidence that no phase of Lueli's development could catch

93

him napping; and he plumed himself on his acuteness in observing that Lueli was growing older every day and was now of an age to assert himself as a young man.

For all that, Mr. Fortune could never quite compass thinking of him as such. Time in this pleasant island where the seasons passed so lightly and where no one ever showed the smallest sense of responsibility was like a long happy afternoon spent under the acacia with the children. However, Lueli was grown up (or would be, the moment he noticed the fact himself) and something would have to be done about it. Something, particularly—for in matters of this sort it is best to go straight to the point—must be done about providing him with a wife.

A Christian wife. And of late he had made several inspections of the village with this end in view, keeping an open eye for all the young women, scanning them as searchingly as Coelebs, artfully devising the like cheese-paring tests for them and pondering which would be the most eligible for conversion and holy matrimony. There were plenty of charming possibles—by now he had quite got over his empirical aversion to them as bevies—though at first sight they seemed more eligible for holy

94

matrimony than for conversion, for one and all
they were smiling, wholesome and inclined to
giggle. But of course convertibility was the
prime consideration. Perhaps by catching his
hare and making a special effort? Mr. Fortune
admitted that during this last year his labours
as a missionary had been growing rather per-
functory.

Not that he loved his flock less. Rather he
loved them more, and to his love was added
(and here was the rub) a considerable amount
of esteem. For seeing the extraordinarily good
hand they made at the business of living to
their own contentment—a business that the wise
consider so extremely laborious and risky—and
reflecting that for all their felicity they yet
contrived to do nobody any harm, he felt some
diffidence in his mission to teach them to do better.

And then he would pull himself up with a
jerk and remember fiercely that they were loose
livers and worshipped idols. Moreover they had
rejected the word of God, and had made their
rejection if anything worse by making it with
such flippancy and unconcern. The seed he scattered had fallen into a soil too rich and easy
so that the weeds sprang up and choked it. Alas,

all their charming good qualities were but a crop of fragrant and exotic groundsel and their innocence was like the pure whiteness and ravishing classical contours of the blossom of the common bindweed, which strangles the corn and looks up from the crime with its exquisite baby face.

Yet after all, he consoled himself by thinking, the apparent reluctance of the Fanuans to become Christians might all be part of God's dealings. God proceeds diversely in divers places, and where His servants had prepared the ground for wheat He may overrule them and set barley. In some islands He may summon the souls with a loud immediate thunderclap; in others He would go about it differently, knowing the secrets of all hearts. God's time is the best. And perhaps it was his intention in Fanua to raise up a people from the marriage of Lueli as He had prepared Himself a people in the seed of Abraham and Sarah. At this thought Mr. Fortune went off into one of his dreams and he grew cold with emotion as he gazed into the future, seeing in a vision Lueli's children and grandchildren and great-grandchildren, mild and blessed, stretching away into the distance like a field of ripened wheat which the wind flows over and the sun shines on. They would remember him, for their fathers would have told them. But no, he thought, there was no need for them to remember him. For it is only the unsatisfied who want to be remembered: old Simeon in the fullness of his joy, beholding the light and the glory had no plea but to depart in peace.

Meanwhile, which girl? Ori's tall daughter, gentle Vaili, or the little plump one who laughed so much that he could never remember her name? It occurred to him that since it was Lueli's wife he was choosing Lueli might well be consulted.

Lueli was out fishing. Mr. Fortune sat till dusk by the spring, thinking out what he would say and choosing his metaphors and turns of speech with unusual pleasure and care as though he were preparing a sermon.

The long shadows had merged into shadow and the western sky was a meditative green when Lueli returned. In one hand he held a glistening net of fish and in the other a bough of fruit, so that he looked like some god of plenty, a brown slip of Demeter's who had not got into the mythology.

Mr. Fortune admired the fish and admired

97

the fruit; but inwardly he admired Lueli more, this beautiful young man smelling of the sea. He gave a little cough and began his speech.

Marriage, he said, was a most excellent thing. It was God's first institution, and in the world's loveliest garden the flowers had asked no better than to be twined into a wreath for the bride. Men's stories commonly end with a marriage, but in God's story the marriage comes at the beginning. The ancient poets when they would celebrate the sun compared him to a bridegroom, the saints could find no tenderer name for Christ than the spouse of the soul, and in the vision of the last things John the Evangelist saw the church descending out of Heaven like a bride, so that God's story which begins with a mortal marriage ends with a marriage too, but an immortal one.

What did Lueli think? Did he not agree that marriage was a good thing?

Lueli nodded. His face wore an admiring and far-away expression, as though he were listening to the harmonium.

Marriage, Mr. Fortune continued, is a gracious act, a bestowal, and a token of man's gratitude to his Maker. When we are happy we needs must give; Lueli himself was always giving, be it fruit or fish, a strand of sea-weed or a flower. These gifts are transient and incomplete; the weed begins to lose its gloss from the moment it is taken out of the ocean, the fish and the fruit (unless, of course, eaten) go bad, the flower is broken from the stem, its petals will discolour and fold up in death; but whoever begets children gives life itself, gives that from which all gifts are drawn.

The procreation of children is the first end for which marriage is ordained. But that was not all. There was also the love of man and woman and the pleasure they had in one another's company. When he was a young man, Mr. Fortune said, he had often wished for a wife to be merry with. Now he was too old to think much of such things but none the less marriage did not seem to him less desirable, for now he understood as he did not and could not in his youth how sweet it would be to have the faithful company of one with whom he had shared his best days if it were only, as a celebrated English Divine once expressed it in a sermon, that he might have someone to whom he could say: "How our shadows lengthen as our sun goes down!"

Mr. Fortune stopped. Lueli's silent consent-

ing and his own thought had led him too far.
He had not meant to introduce such serious con-
siderations into a discourse on marriage, and the
mournful sound of his own voice alone in the
shadow of night suddenly revealed to him that
he was sorrowful, although he had not thought
he was.

"Tell me, Lueli, have you thought at all
about whom you would prefer?"

"Vaili is a nice girl and her father would
give her a good dowry——"

Lueli pressed up the tip of his nose with the
tip of his finger and spoke in a soft considering
voice.

"Or there is Fuma, or Lepe who loves singing. But I think Vaili would suit you best, so
you had better marry her."

"I marry! No, no, Lueli, you are mistaken,
I was not talking of myself but of you. It is
your marriage I was thinking about."

"Oh! Were you?"

"Wouldn't you like a wife, Lueli? As you
were saying, Vaili is a nice girl. She is gentle
and fond of children, we could soon teach her
to become a Christian if we gave our minds
to it. I'm sure you could be very happy with
Vaili."

A decided shake of the head.

"Fuma, then."

Another shake.

"Well, what about Lepe or Tialua?"

Mr. Fortune proceeded to recite the names of all the girls on the island, feeling not very respectable as he did so, but going steadfastly on because he was in for it now, he could not go back on his own sermon. But he might as well have recited the Kings of Israel and Judah or the Queens consort of England from Matilda of Flanders down to Adelaide of Saxe-Meiningen for all the effect it had on Lueli, who sat beside him listening decorously as though to a lesson and silently waving away each one of Mr. Fortune's nominees.

"But, Lueli, if you don't approve of any of these, whom do you want?"

A terrible possibility had flashed upon him. Suppose like the traditional young man, Lueli had placed his affections on some mature married woman? What steps should he take, indeed what steps could he take? He would not even have public opinion on his side.

"I don't want anyone. I am quite happy as I am."

"But Lueli, you are young and vigorous.

This is not natural and I don't think it is at all advisable. Why St. Paul himself—" And Mr. Fortune gave a short summary of St. Paul's views on the marrying or burning question, toning them down a little, for privately he considered the saint's conclusions a trifle acrid. But there was no shaking Lueli, who continued to asseverate that he found chastity an easier matter than St. Paul supposed, and in any case preferable to the nuisance of taking a wife.

It seemed rather odd and improbable to Mr. Fortune. But he let the matter drop and did not speak of it again. Lueli would change his tune all in good time no doubt. Meanwhile things could go on as before, and certainly nothing could be pleasanter. Of course, he was properly desirous to see the beginnings of that Christian family and he was much looking forward to becoming a godfather. He had already settled that since the proper consecrated kind of mugs were unprocurable the first child should have the tea-pot and the second the sovereign he still kept for luck. After that he supposed he would have to sacrifice the magnifying glass and the tuning fork, and after that again—well, he still had time to think about it. Indeed at present even the tea-pot seemed indefinitely postponed.

He was puzzled by Lueli, but he was not uneasy about him; when he went off by himself he did not speculate as to what he was up to, nor ask strategic questions on his return. He trusted the boy and he also trusted himself. He did not think he could be deceived in Lueli.

And so things went kindly and easily on till the day when he was to find out his mistake.

It was very hot weather. Mr. Fortune had been suffering from a severe headache, and had spent the whole day lying down in the shade with wet cloths on his head. About sundown he decided to go for a short stroll, hoping that the dusk and the cool airs from the sea would refresh him. He called for Lueli to come too, but Lueli was nowhere about, so he set forth alone, crossing the dell and going down toward the sea. As he went he admired the brilliance of the afterglow, a marvellous rose-coloured bloom that seemed to hang on the air like a cloud of the finest metallic dust. Perhaps his eyes were weakened by headache and so more sensitive to light than usual; but as he roamed up and down the shadowy strand, at each turn that brought him to face the west he marvelled, thinking that in all his evenings at Fanua he had never beheld the sky so vibrating with colour nor so slow to fade; for sunsets in the tropics are fleeting things, but to-night there was a strange steadfastness in the west. He admired it so much that is was not possible for him to admire it for very long, and there was still light in the sky as he turned homeward.

Ordinarily he kept to the same routes as faithfully as though they had been ruled for him with red ink. But to-night, lost in thoughts of he knew not what, he strayed from his direction and found himself approaching a little grove of coco-palms. They grew prettily together, laced with creepers and thickened with an undergrowth of ferns; there was something about the innocence of their arrangement which reminded him of an English copse, and the resemblance was increased by a little path that turned and twisted its way in among them. But in an English copse even the slenderest path is wide enough for two lovers to walk it with their arms about each other, while this path was so narrow that it was clearly the path of one who visited the thicket alone.

A parrot flew off from a bough above his head, uttering a loud cry. Mr. Fortune roused himself from his dream. He was not in an

English copse, looking for bluebells and being careful not to tread on a nightingale's nest, he was in a grove of coco-palms on the island of Fanua, an island in the midst of the Pacific ocean like an island in a story book. And he was looking for——? He was not looking for anything; for in all his time at Fanua though he admired the flowers he had rarely picked any. It did not occur to him to do so. One picks only the flowers that one learned to pick as a child— cowslips and primroses and cuckoo-pint, and pale starwort that grows in the dusty summer hedge and fades before one can carry it home.

Lueli was always picking flowers. Perhaps he came here for them, perhaps he had been along this path but an hour ago? At any rate some flower gatherer had; for lying at his feet Mr. Fortune observed a dark-coloured blossom like a stain. He stooped and picked it up. Yes, it was freshly gathered, it had not begun to wither yet, but it was moist with dew and felt cold and forsaken.

Presently Mr. Fortune came on a trail of lilac-flowered creeper caught up on a fern. He disentangled this and carried it along with him.

"Extravagant creature!" he said; for now he

felt sure that he was on Lueli's track. "I could make myself a bouquet out of what he spills and scatters."

He still followed the path, wondering what next he would pick up. A little further on he perceived a whole garland lying on a patch of greensward. He was in the heart of the little wood and here the path seemed to end.

"I declare that he's still child enough to be playing at houses. And this is the young man I've been trying to find a wife for!"

It looked exactly as though Lueli had been playing at house. The ferns and bushes were hung with trailing sprays of blossom which looped them into a pretence of being walls, and in the midst beside the garland was a platter arranged with fruits and leaves.

"What a child!" exclaimed the priest. "Yet after all it may not be Lueli. Why should I be so sure that this is his fancy-work?"

In an instant he was to be made quite sure. Something slim and dusky and motionless was reared up behind the platter of fruit. He looked closer. It was dreadfully familiar. He snatched it up and stared close into its face, a face he had seen before. And trampling on the garland he stood glaring at Lueli's idol, which looked back at him with flowers behind its ears.

It was quite obvious, quite certain. There was no chance of being mistaken, no hope of doubt. For all these years Lueli had been playing a double game, betraying him, feigning to be a Christian, and in secret, in the reality of secretness, worshipping an idol.

"It's my fault," said the priest, speaking aloud because of his desperate loneliness. "Not his at all, nor yours either," and he gave the idol a sort of compassionate shake.

"I have deluded myself wilfully, I have built my house on the sand. . . ."

"I have forgotten the fear of God," he went on. "All this time I have gone on pretending that religion is a pleasant, is a gentle thing, a game for good children."

"But it is an agony!" he suddenly shouted out.

There was no echo. The sultry twilight was closing in on him like a dark fleece. He could scarcely see the idol now, but in his mind's eye he could see it, a face coldly and politely attentive, and the narrow polished shoulders over which a doll's necklace slipped and sidled as it shook with his trembling hands.

"It is torments, wounds, mutilation, and death. It is exile and weariness. It is strife—

an endless strife—it is bewilderment and fear and trembling. It is despair."

Turning abruptly he left the thicket by the path which had led him in, and stumbling in the dark and feeling his body heavy and cold in the hot night he made his way to the hut.

It was all dark; but that was no reason why Lueli should not be within, for he had been so often warned to handle the lamp carefully that he was a coward about it and never touched it if he could avoid doing so.

Mr. Fortune threw down the idol and lit the lamp from his tinder-box. Then he looked round. Lueli was curled up on his mat. He had been asleep and now he opened his eyes and looked drowsily at his friend. Mr. Fortune said nothing. He stood in the centre of the hut under the hanging lamp and waited for Lueli to notice the idol.

Lueli parted his lips. He was just about to speak when he saw what lay on the ground. He raised his eyes to Mr. Fortune's countenance, for a moment he put on a confused smile, then with an ill-feigned yawn he turned over and pretended to have fallen asleep again.

"Deceit," said Mr. Fortune, as though he were reading from a note-book.

A faint grunt answered him.

"Lueli, my poor Lueli, this is useless. You can't get out of it like this. Get up and tell me what it is that I have found."

Lueli sat up. The pupils of his eyes were still distended by sleep and this gave him a frightened look; but his demeanour was perfectly· calm.

"That?"

He shook his head as if to say that he really couldn't tell what it was.

"Look again."

Mr. Fortune spoke curtly, but it was from pure sorrow.

"It is an idol."

"Yes, and it is your idol."

Lueli gave a sigh of distress. Mr. Fortune knew exactly how much that was worth. Lueli hated any unpleasantness.

"You don't ask me how I came by it. I found it in a thicket near the beach, the lonely one. And there were flowers round it, and offerings of fruit, and look, there are flowers stuck behind its ears."

"So there are."

"Is this your doing? Why do I ask you, for I know it is. Lueli, you mustn't lie to me. I im-

plore you not to lie. Is this your doing, have you
been worshipping this object?"

"I picked the flowers."

Mr. Fortune groaned. Then he sat down like
one who foresees a long and weariful business
before him. Lueli edged himself a little nearer.
He had rumpled up his brow into a grimace of
condolence, he looked like a beautiful and sym-
pathetic marmoset.

He said in a voice at once tender and sly:

"But why are you unhappy? I have done
nothing, it is only my idol, and I just happened
to pick it a few flowers. That is all."

"Listen. I will tell you why I am unhappy.
When I came to Fanua I came to teach you
not to worship idols but to worship God. I came
to teach you all, but the others would have none
of me. You were my only convert, you received
my teaching, I thought you loved it, and I
trusted you. Now I have found out my mistake. If you worship your idol still I am to
blame. It is my fault. If I had done my duty
by you you would have known better. But I
have not shown you the true God, so you have
kept to the old one, the false one, a wooden
thing, a worship so false that you can treat him
like a toy. As I came back to-night I was

tempted with the thought that perhaps after all your fault was only childishness. And for a moment (to spare myself and you) I had half a mind to pretend to God that your idol was only a doll. But we will have none of that."

Now he spoke sternly, and at the last words he beat one fist against the other. Lueli started.

"I blame myself, I say, not you. I should have been on my guard. When I saw that thing four years ago I should have acted then. But I shut my eyes (I am most horribly to blame) and now, see what has come of it. You are in fault too, for you have been deceiving me. But I know you are rather cowardly and very affectionate; your deceitfulness after all is not so surprising."

He could have gone on talking like this for some time and finding it soothing, but he knew by experience that Lueli would find it soothing too. He raised his eyes from his heavily folded hands and looked at the boy. Sure enough, there was the familiar expression, the lulled face of one who listens to a powerful spell.

He stopped short, nerved himself to deliver the blow and said in a slow dull voice:

"You must destroy your idol. You had better burn it."

With a vehement gesture of refusal Lueli sprang to his feet.

"Burn it," repeated the priest.

Such a wild and affronted antagonism defied him from the tautened brown body and the unswerving, unbeholding gaze that for a moment the priest was appalled. But his looks gave back defiance for defiance. They bore the other's down, and averting his eyes Lueli gave a sudden shrug and made as though to walk out of the hut.

Mr. Fortune was between him and the door. He jumped up and barred the line of retreat. Lueli wavered. Then he went back to his corner and sat down without a word. Mr. Fortune half expected him to weep, but he did nothing so obliging.

For a good hour Mr. Fortune talked on, commanding, reasoning, expostulating, explaining, persuading, threatening. Lueli never answered him, never even looked at him. He sat with downcast eyes in utter stubbornness and immobility.

The night was sultry and absolutely still. Mr. Fortune dripped with sweat, he felt as though he were heaving enormous boulders into a bottomless pit. He continued to heave his

words into silence, a silence only broken by the
hissing of the lamp, or the creak of his chair
as he changed from one uneasy position to another, but the pauses grew longer between each
sentence. He was weary, and at his wit's end.
But he could see nothing for it but to go on
talking. And now he became so oppressed by
the silence into which he spoke that he could
foresee a moment when he would have to go on
talking because he would be afraid to hold his
tongue.

A frightful imagination took possession of
him: that Lueli was become like his idol, a
handsome impassive thing of brown wood, that
had ears and heard not, that had no life in its
heart. Would nothing move him? He would
have been thankful for a look of hate, for a
curse or an insult. But with the same show of
inanimate obstinacy Lueli continued to bend
his look upon the ground, a figure too austere
to be sullen, too much withdrawn into itself to
be defiant.

Mr. Fortune heard himself say at the top of
his voice: "Lueli! Don't you hear me?"

It seemed that his outcry had broken the
spell. Lueli suddenly looked up and began to
listen, to listen with such strained, absorbed,

animal attention that Mr. Fortune found himself listening too. There was a sound: a sound like a violent gust of wind strangely sweeping through the motionless night. It came rapidly, it came near, brushing its way through the treetops. Like an actual angry presence the wind came vehemently into the hut and as though an invisible hand had touched it Mr. Fortune saw the hanging lamp begin to sway. It swayed faster and faster, widening its sweep at every oscillation; and while he stared at it in a stupor of amazement he felt the earth give a violent twitch under his feet as though it were hitting up at him and he was thrown to the ground. There was a noise of rending and bellowing, the lamp gave a last frantic leap, again he felt the ground buffet him like the horns of a bull and then with a crash and a spurt of fire the roof of the hut caved in.

At the same moment he felt something large and heavy topple across his body.

He could not move and he could not think. He saw flames rising up around him and heard the crackle of the dried thatch. Again the ground began to quiver and writhe beneath him, and suddenly he knew what was happening—an earthquake!

The bulk that lay on top of him was the harmonium. He was pinned beneath it—presently the flames would reach him and he would be burnt to death.

He felt no kind of fear or emotion, only a calm certainty as to what was happening, and with it a curious detached satisfaction at being able to understand it all so well. The flames would enclose him and he would be burnt to death, unless the ground opened first and swallowed him up. Then he remembered Lueli. What of him? He struggled again, but he could not get out from under the harmonium. The struggle reminded him that he was a human being, not only an intelligence but a creature defencelessly sentient that must perish by fire. Fear came on him, and self-pity, and with it a sort of pique; for he said to himself: "I know now he never cared for me. He has made off and left me to burn, just what I should expect." And at the same moment he heard himself cry out: "Save yourself, Lueli! Be quick, child! Never mind me, I am all right." And then, seeing Lueli bending over him, he said in a voice of command: "Lueli, I tell you to save yourself. Get out of this while there's time."

He saw Lueli in the light of the flames, he

saw him put his shoulder against the harmonium and begin to heave it up; he saw the muscles leap out along the thrusting body—all with a sort of anger and impatience because his friend would not attend to what he was saying. Even when it was jolted backward and he was freed he lay where he had fallen, half-stunned, with no definite thought except to compel Lueli to obey him and get away before the next tremor sent the whole hut crashing down on them.

He felt Lueli put his arms round his shoulders, shaking him and hauling him on to his feet, and he noticed with surprise how stern the boy looked, not frightened, but extraordinarily stern, like a stranger, like an angel. The earth began to quake again, another sheaf of thatch slid from the roof and the flames leaped up to seize upon it. Mr. Fortune suddenly came out of his stupor. Stumbling and losing his footing on the wavering floor he caught hold of Lueli's arm and together they ran out of the hut.

Three times in crossing the dell they were thrown to the earth. There was something horribly comic in this inability to stand upright. It was as though they were being tossed in a blanket. They did not speak to each other; all

thought of speech was forbidden by the appalling
novelty of the uproar that was going on, rumblings and bellowings underground, trees beating against each other or crashing to the ground,
the cries of terror-struck creatures. Lueli
dragged him on, hastening toward the mountain. There was a little path that led up by the
ravine, difficult to mount at any time and more
difficult still in an earthquake.

"Why do you go this way?" Mr. Fortune
asked, when the tremor had subsided enough
for him to be able to remember how to speak.
Lueli turned on him a face of terror.

"The sea," he said. "The sea."

Mr. Fortune had forgotten the sea. Now he
remembered what he had read in books of ad-
venture as a boy: how after an earthquake
comes a tidal wave, a wall of water frantically
hurling itself upon the land. And not daring
to look behind him he followed Lueli up the
steep path as though the sea were at his heels.

At last they came out upon a little grassy
platform, overlooking the ravine. They were
only just in time, for the earthquake began
again. They sat side by side, holding on to one
another. Mr. Fortune discovered that it was a
brilliant and impassive moonlight night. He

looked toward the ocean. It seemed strangely calm, incredibly vast, more solid than the tormented earth. A glittering path of silver across it reflected the moon.

They were close to the cataract. To-night, instead of the usual steady roar of falling water, the noise was coming in curious gouts of sound, now loud, now almost nothing. He turned his eyes and saw the slender column of falling water all distorted, and flapping like a piece of muslin in a draught. For some reason this sight was overwhelmingly piteous and a sort of throe hollowed him as if he were going to cry.

At every shock thousands of birds flew up from the tossing tree-tops. In wild excitement they circled overhead, flying in droves, sweeping past with a whirr of innumerable wings, soaring higher and higher, then suddenly diving aslant, shot from the wake of their own vortex. Their continual angry clamour, passionate and derisive, swayed above the uproar of trampling earth and clashing forest. One bird came volleying so close to Mr. Fortune that he saw its beak flash in the moonlight and put up his hand to shield his face. As it passed it screamed in his ear like a railway whistle. He thought: "I should like to scream like that."

Although he and Lueli sat holding on to each other, Mr. Fortune had no sense of companionship. In this appalling hour there did not seem to be anyone alive save himself. He was the Last Man, alone in a universe which had betrayed him, abandoned on the face of an earth which had failed under his feet. He was isolated even from himself. There was no Mr. Fortune now, a missionary who had been a bank-clerk, an Englishman and a member of the Church of England. Such a one would have been behaving quite differently. At the best he might have been behaving much better, he might have been in the village, keeping troth with his fellow-men; at the least he would have been trembling for his own skin and calling on God. But this man sat on the reeling mountainside with but one sensation: a cold-hearted excitement, a ruthless attentive craving that at the height of horror would welcome another turn of the screw, another jab of the spur, another record broken.

The shocks were now coming so continuously that it was scarcely possible to say when one followed another; but he went on keeping count and comparing them, and if they seemed to be slackening off he was disappointed. He sat with his eyes shut, for so he could both feel and hear more unmitigatedly. At intervals he looked out seaward for the coming of the tidal wave. But the sea was always calm, as coldly calm as himself and a great deal more solid. "Yet it must come," he told himself. "It is certain to come." And after a terrific shock, accompanied by sounds of rending and shattering as though the whole island were splitting asunder, he thought with certainty: "It will come now," and opened his eyes once more.

Something had happened. There was a difference in the air, in the colour of the night. Had dawn come already? His faculties were so cramped with attention that he could scarcely receive a new sensation, still less analyse it. Yet he felt that there was something he must account for, some discrepancy between this light and the light of dawn. The sun rose—yes, the sun rose in the east, over the sea: but this light seemed to come from behind him. He turned and saw the sky lit up with the light of fire.

"The mountain is on fire!" he cried out. And at the sound of his own words he suddenly understood what had happened. The mountain was on fire. Its ancient fires had come back to it, Fanua was once more an active volcano.

Below the bed of the cold and heavy sea, below the foundations of the great deep, into an unimaginable hell of energy and black burning those fires had withdrawn. They had rejoined the imprisoned original frenzy that lies in the heart of the earth, working and wallowing in unknown tides, and once more the fiery spring had mounted, revolting against the encompassing pressure, fumbling in darkness, melting its way, flooding along its former channels until now it flared on the crest of the island, brightening and brightening upon the sky, a glow of such intense and vivid rose-colour that by contrast the moonlight turned to an icily-piercing blue. Cloud upon cloud of smoke rolled upwards and at every fresh surge of fire the vault of heaven appeared to grow more vast and haughty, and the stars seemed recoiling into space. The mountain shouted and bellowed as though it were triumphing because its fires had come back to it.

Mr. Fortune leapt to his feet. He waved his arms, he stood on tip-toe in order to see better. Though the next moment might engulf him he was going to make the most of this. But there was no need to be so provident, so economical. This bonfire had been preparing for decades, it would not burn out in a minute or two. Realizing this he sat down again and relinquished himself to an entire and passive contemplation, almost lulled by the inexhaustible procession of fire and smoke, warming his mind at the lonely terrific beauty of a mountain burning by night amid an ocean.

Clouds began to gather at daybreak. Only a pallor showed where the sun groped upwards among them, and the sea which but a few hours ago had looked so lustrous, and solid like a floor of onyx, was now pale and weltering.

The earthquake seemed to be over; sometimes the ground gave a sort of a twitch and a tremble like an animal that dreams a bad dream; but this happened at longer and longer intervals and each disturbance was fainter than the last. Except for the plume of foul smoke that issued from the crater and sagged over the mountain-side as it was checked by the morning airs there was nothing to distinguish this daybreak from any other, unless, thought Mr. Fortune, that it was a peculiarly dreary one.

He was chilled with watching, and oppressed with the indigestion common to those who have sat up all night. He was also bruised with so much falling about, and his ribs ached from being crushed under the harmonium. But his hand gently on Lueli's arm. There was no response. Lueli didn't even turn his eyes.

"He is tired out," thought the priest. "That is why he looks so miserable." He said aloud: "Wake up, Lueli, you will make yourself ill if you lie there any longer so still on the cold ground. Wake up. Rouse yourself. It is all over now." And he gave him an encouraging slap on the shoulder.

At last Lueli sighed and stretched himself and turned and met Mr. Fortune's anxious gaze.

"I think the earthquake is over," he remarked in an everyday voice.

"Just what I said a minute ago," thought Mr. Fortune. "But he doesn't know I said it. What can he have been thinking of that he didn't hear me?"

He still felt slightly worried about the boy.

"We had better walk about a little," he said. "Ow! I've got cramp."

Taking Lueli's arm he staggered down the little rocky path. The morning was cold and now it began to rain. The rain was dirty rain, full of smuts and fine grit from the volcano. It might have been raining in London or Manchester.

Exercise soon restored Mr. Fortune to an

ordinary frame of mind. He looked with interested horror at the wood they passed through.
Many trees were uprooted or hung tottering
with their roots half out of the ground, the
shrubs and grass were crushed and trampled,
boughs and torn creepers were scattered everywhere. It was as though some savage beast had
run amuck through the glades, tearing and hav-
ocking and rooting up the ground with its horns.
Lueli picked up a dead parrot, and once they
skirted by a swarm of angry bees. Their hive
had been broken in the fall of its tree, the honey-
comb was scattered on the grass and the affronted insects were buzzing hither and thither,
angrier than ever because now the rain was
making its way through the dishevelled green
roof.

"But it will soon quench them," thought Mr.
Fortune. "And if some bees and some parrots
are the only deaths by this earthquake we shall
be well out of it."

He was uneasy about the villagers, all the
more so because he had run away from them in
their hour of peril. Also he wanted to talk to
someone about the stream of lava which he
knew would soon flow down from the crater.
Provided it only flows to the south, he thought.

He questioned Lueli but could learn nothing; Lueli had never been in an earthquake before, he had heard the old men of the island talking about them but the last earthquake had happened long before his day.

On nearing the village Mr. Fortune heard a great hub-bub, but it was impossible to discover from the noise of everyone talking at once whether they were lamenting or merely excited; all he could conclude was that at any rate they were not all dead.

When he appeared, with Lueli following sedately behind, a crowd of gesticulating islanders rushed forward, all waving their arms and shouting. The thought leapt up in his mind: "Suppose they think that *I* am responsible for this earthquake? Perhaps they will kill me to appease the mountain!" He had never felt less in the mood for martyrdom. The last twelve hours had given him more than enough to cope with. Yet even if the fervour of his faith were lacking he could make a shift to die decently: and he stiffened himself and went forward. But Lueli? Suppose they wanted to martyr him too? No! That he would not allow. While there was a kick left in him he would see to that. He glanced back as though to reassure him, but as

he caught sight of him he remembered that
Lueli was not a Christian, nor ever had been
one. What a sell if they should sacrifice him
before there was time to explain! Well, this
made it even more urgent a matter to defend
him: martyrdom was one thing, miscarriage of
justice quite another.

But Mr. Fortune need not have been agitated.
The islanders had no intention but to welcome
him and Lueli, and to rejoice round them over
their safety; which they did with the pleasanter
excitement and conviction since naturally, in
the emotions of the night they had not given
them a thought till now.

Half smothered and quite deafened, Mr.
Fortune pushed through the throng, saying:
"Where is Ori?" For having lived so long on
the island he had fallen into the proper respect
for a chief, and depended on Ori rather more
than he would have liked to admit. "He is almost like another European,"—so the priest
explained to himself. At this juncture Ori was
behaving very much like an European, for he
was partaking of one of those emergency break-
fasts, sketchy in form but extremely solid and
comprehensive in content, with which the white
races consummate and, as it were, justify any

fly-by-night catastrophe. Seeing Mr. Fortune he politely invited him to sit down and take a share. "But the flow of lava?" enquired Mr. Fortune, wiping his mouth. "Do you think it will come this way?" Ori took another handful of stirabout. "There are no signs of it so far and if it comes this way it will not come here yet."

"But do you think it will come this way?"

"My god says, No."

When breakfast was finished Ori got up and went off with the other men of consequence to make an inquisition into the damage done by the pigs. They had come bolting down from the woods and wrought even more serious havoc than the earthquake, which had only shaken down a house or two, whereas the pigs had trespassed into every enclosure and eaten all the provisions. Mr. Fortune felt a little slighted that he was not invited to go too. Apparently Ori did not quite regard him as another Fanuan. "Oh well," he said. "Perhaps they meant it politely, seeing that I had not finished my breakfast." But though he felt as if he were hungry he had no real appetite, and rising he prepared to walk back to his hut.

It was as though the earthquake had literally

shaken his wits. All his recollections were dis-
lodged and tumbled together, he knew they
were there somewhere, but he could not find
them, just as he had mislaid the discovery of
overnight until, turning to view Lueli as a possible martyr, he beheld and recognized him as
the idolater he was and always had been. Now
he was walking to the hut in the same kind of
oblivion. He must have remembered the lamp
tossing its flame up to the roof, the burning
sheaves of thatch falling down around him, for
he had a very clear vision of Lueli's face bending over him, so violently modelled by the
flames that it had looked like the face, sad and
powerful, of a stranger, of an angel. But his
thoughts went no further; and even when the
smell of charred wood came sadly to his nostrils through the falling rain he did not put two
and two together.

"I wonder if those pigs have messed up my
place too," he said. A sigh out of the air answered him. He had not noticed till then that
Lueli was following.

"Poor Lueli, you must be so tired!" There
was no answer and still the boy lagged behind.
He must be tired indeed. Mr. Fortune stopped.
He was about to speak once more, bidding Lueli

to lean on him and take heart, when suddenly
the boy shot past him, running desperately, and
whispering to himself as he ran as though he
were imploring his own mind.

Mr. Fortune hastened after him. Would all
this strangeness, this bewilderment, this nightmare of familiar living confounded and turned
backward never come to an end? He hastened
on into the smell of burning and pulling aside
the drooping fronds of a banana tree which,
uprooted, had fallen and lay across the pathway
like a screen, he beheld the ruins of the hut.

One wall was still standing, a few pale
flames licking wistfully over it. The rest was
charred logs and hummocks of grey ash, siz-
zling under the rain—for now it was raining
more and more heavily. Looking round on the
devastation he began to recognize the remains
of his belongings. Those shreds of tinder were
his clothes. That scrap of shrivelled leather,
that wasting impalpable bulk of feathery print
was his Bible; there lay the medicine chest and
there the sewing-machine, and this, this intricate ruin of molten metal tubes, charred rubber
and dislocated machinery was the harmonium,
its scorched ivory keys strewed round about it
like teeth fallen from a monstrous head.

131

Lueli was there, but he seemed to have no thought for the unfortunate priest amid the ruins of his home. Wading among the hot ashes, crouching close to the wreckage, turning over this and that with rapid and trembling hands, Lueli was searching with desperate anxiety for—Mr. Fortune knew not what. At length he gave a bitter cry and cast himself upon the ground.

Instantly Mr. Fortune was kneeling beside him, patting his shoulder, trying to lift the averted head.

"What is it, Lueli? What is it, my dear, dear friend?"

Lueli sat up and turned on him a face discoloured and petrified into an expression of such misery that he could hardly endure to look at it.

"What is it? Are you hurt? Are you ill?"

The expression never changed.

"Are you frightened, Lueli? Has it upset you to find our home burnt to the ground? But never mind! We will soon have another, it is nothing to grieve for."

He would have said that Lueli did not hear him, so unmoving he sat, so utterly aloof, but that at these last words a very slight smile of scorn quivered on the dry lips.

Then Mr. Fortune remembered. He hung

132

his head and when he spoke again it was with the grave voice in which we address the bereaved.

"Is it your god you were looking for? Is he gone?"

Lueli did not answer. But it was clear that he had both heard and understood, for he fixed his eyes on the priest's face with the look of an animal which knows itself at man's mercy but does not know what man intends to do to it.

"My poor Lueli! Is that it? . . . Is it so dreadful? Yes, I know it must be, I know, I know. I would do anything to comfort you, but I cannot think now, I can only tell you how I pity you with my whole heart. I do, indeed I do. Believe me, though I told you to burn your god, yet at this moment, if it were possible for me, I think I would even give it to you again."

He spoke very slowly, scarcely daring to lift his gaze to the sorrow which sat beside him, not answering, not crying out, meek with the meekness of despair. And still Lueli listened, and still looked, with his expression wavering between timidity and antagonism.

"Lueli, I spoke very harshly to you last night, not like a Christian, not as one sad human being should speak to another. In blas-

pheming against your god I blasphemed against
my own. And now I can't comfort you. I don't
deserve to. I can only sit beside you and be
sorry."

Lueli never answered and Mr. Fortune acted
his last words, sitting mournfully beside him in
the rain. After an hour or so Lueli began to
topple forward, then suddenly he lay down and
fell asleep.

Now Mr. Fortune had time to think, and
though he was dog-tired think he must. For
after awhile Lueli would wake again, and then
the missionary must have some settled reasonable comfort for him, some plan of consolation.
On the face of it nothing could be clearer. He
should say something of this sort: "Your god,
Lueli, was only made of wood, perishable and
subject to accidents, like man who is made of
flesh. He is now burnt, and his ashes are lost
among the other ashes. Now will you not see
that my God is a better God than yours, and
turn to Him? For my God is from everlasting,
even though the earth shake He cannot be
moved."

Yes, that was the sort of thing to say, but
he felt a deep reluctance to saying it. It seemed
ungentlemanly to have such a superior invulner-

able God, part of that European conspiracy which opposes gun-boats to canoes and rifles to bows and arrows, which showers death from the mountains upon Indian villages, which rounds up the negro in an empire and tricks him of his patrimony.

Mr. Fortune remembered the Man of Sorrows. Would Lueli accept in the place of his wooden god a God that had once been made flesh? In the old days Lueli had enjoyed hearing about Jesus, though Mr. Fortune had always suspected him of preferring Joshua. Many, very many must have taken Jesus to their hearts out of pity; following the example of the woman who washed His feet although to her they were most likely but the feet of a wayfaring man. But it was rare to find a Polynesian accepting Him for these mortal motives, they themselves were not sorrowful enough. Probably despite the loss of his god Lueli would still prefer the more robust and stirring character of Joshua.

The trumpet that shall awaken the dead with the sanction of the resurrection is louder than all the rams' horns that blew down Jericho. As an honest priest it was Mr. Fortune's duty to preach, not only Christ crucified but also Christ arisen to comfort His followers awhile with neighbourly humanity ere He ascended to His Father. If this were all, it might suit Lueli very well: but in a twinkling it would lead him on to the Trinity, a mysterious sign revolving in the heavens from everlasting, a triangle that somehow is also a sphere. And so he was back again where he started from, embarrassed with a God so superior to poor Lueli's that to insist upon him now would be heartless boasting, would be exploiting an unfair advantage, wouldn't be cricket.

"If I were a proper missionary,"—he burst out in a cross voice. And then with a wry grin he added: "It doesn't look as though I were any sort of missionary. Lord, what a mess I've made of it!"

He had indeed. The mess amid which he sat was nothing to it. Disconsolately, he looked at his watch. It had stopped. In the stress of overnight he had forgotten to wind it up, and now it recorded the epoch at which his last link with European civilization had been snapped— eight hours thirty-five minutes. It could not be much later than that now. But a miss is as good as a mile, and for the rest of his sojourn on the island, for the rest of his life maybe, he would not know what o'clock it was. This circum-

stance, not serious in itself and not to be compared with the loss of the medicine chest or
his books, upset him horribly. He felt frightened,
he felt as small and as desperate as a child lost.
"I must set it as best I can," he thought. "After
all, time is a convention, just like anything else.
My watch will measure out my days and re-
mind me to be up and doing just as well though
it be a little askew. And no doubt I shall die
at my appointed hour however erroneously I
reckon to it."

But what time was it? The sky was overcast,
he could not guess by the sun and he could not
guess by his own time-feeling either, for his
body had lost touch with ordinary life. He sat
debating between nine-seventeen, five past ten,
ten forty-three, eleven-twenty—indecisive times
which all seemed reasonably probable, and noon
exactly, which was bracing and decisive, a good
moment to begin a new era—but too good to be
true. At last he settled on ten twenty-five; but
even so he still delayed, for he felt a supersti-
tious reluctance to move the hands and so to
destroy the last authentic witness his watch
could bear him. Five minutes, he judged, had
been spent in this weak-minded dallying: so res-
olutely he set the hands to ten-thirty and wound

the poor machine up. It began to tick, inno-
cently, obediently. It had set out on its fraudu-
lent career.

It was a good watch, painstaking and punc-
tual, its voice was confident, it had an honest
face; but henceforth its master had lost his
trust in it, and though he wore it (like a wife)
at bed and board and wound it up regularly
and hung it on a tree when he went bathing,
yet he never could feel it was his true wife
(watch, I mean) again.

Still Lueli slept.

"I make all this fuss," thought Mr. Fortune.
"I even feel helpless and abandoned, because
I have lost my reckoning of time. How much
worse to lose one's God!"

Thus the watch diversion over and done
with, and the new time being ten-thirty-one, he
was back on the old problem. What could he
do for poor Lueli who had lost his god? "And
it was for me that he lost it," he thought, with
a poignancy of feeling that was almost irrita-
tion. "He might have picked up his god and
run out of the hut with it, but he would not
leave me under the harmonium." It was heroic,
desperately heroic. . . . Yet there might have
been time to save both? A god that could be

picked up in one hand. Had Lueli in the flurry of the moment forgotten that the idol lay on the floor of the hut? But No, one would not forget one's god, thought he, even in an earthquake.

Now he could understand why Lueli had seemed so cold in the early morning, so aloof and unlike his usual self. When he had lain staring out to sea with that strange expression he had been tasting what it feels like to be without a god. And when they approached the hut that was why he had lagged behind until the last explosion of hope had sent him running to seek his god among the wood-ashes. Now he was asleep. But he would not sleep much longer. Already he had stirred once or twice, and sighed, as those do who must soon awaken. And still Mr. Fortune had not settled how to deal with him when he awoke. Would the Man of Sorrows fit his sorrowful case, He who had once cried out, *"Eloi, Eloi, lama sabacthani?"* Or would it be better to try Jehovah, a tribal character whose voice was in the clouds, whose arrows stuck very fast? The worst of it was that Lueli knew all about them already. For three years he had been living on the terms of the greatest intimacy with them, he was even at

home with the Trinity. And so all that Mr.
Fortune could tell him now would be but a
twice-told tale; and that was not likely to be
of much effect, for Polynesians are fickle, they
tire as easily as children and must be bribed with
novelties.

Mr. Fortune grew increasingly despondent.
He was even growing bored, and more and
more quickly he turned over in his mind the
various expedients of Godhead which might ap-
peal to Lueli, like a woman tossing over a piece-
bag in search of something she cannot find. The
blue print, the grey merino, the long and ever
more tangled trail of metal lace, a scrap of
corduroy: none of these is what she looks for,
and what she looks for is not there.

"I can do nothing," he cried out; and then
an inner voice finishing the quotation for him
added, "without Thee."

Of course he could do nothing without God.
Why had he not thought of that before? Why,
instead of vain thinking, hadn't he prayed?

He looked about him. He was alone in a
mesh of rain. For leagues around the rain was
falling, falling upon the quenched ashes of his
homestead where were mingled and quenched
too the ashes of Lueli's god, falling upon the

motionless forest, falling upon the moving
ocean, on that vast watery and indivisible web
of tides and currents, falling everywhere with
an equal and unstaying pressure. Only upon the
newly-open mouth of the pit was the rain not
falling, for there the flames rushed up and
caught and consumed it.

There had been an earthquake and now it
was raining. Both events were equally natural,
equally accountable for, equally inevitable.
There was nowhere any room for chance; no
happening from the greatest to the least could
be altered or provoked or turned aside. And why
should he specify into greatest or least? In
causation there is no great or small. He himself
was as great as the mountain, as little as the
least of the ashes of Lueli's god.

Still he looked about him. But he was not
looking for anything now nor did he need to
raise his eyes to heaven or close them before
any presence unseen. The God who had walked
with him upon the island had gone. He had ascended in the flames that had burst roaring and
devouring from the mountain-top, and hiding
His departure in clouds of smoke, He had gone
up and was lost in space.

Mr. Fortune no longer believed in a God.

It had all happened quite quietly, just like that. Once he put out his hand as though to arrest something that was floating away out of reach, but in a moment it dropped again. And there it was before him, resting upon his knees, the hand of a man who didn't any longer believe in a God, with fingers idly patting out a slow and flagging rhythm, tick-tock like a time-piece that is running down. The real time-piece went on nimbly enough, it was now (he noticed) five minutes to eleven of the new era. If his diary had not been burnt he could have mentioned in it with impressive accuracy: "At 10:54 A. M. (N. T.) I ceased to believe in God." This quaint fancy gave him pleasure.

How differently to Lueli was he taking his loss. The reason must be that Lueli though losing his god had kept his faith. Lueli had lost something real, like losing an umbrella; he had lost it with frenzy and conviction. But *his* loss was utter and retrospective, a lightning-flash loss which had wiped out a whole life-time of having. In fact the best way of expressing it, though it sounded silly and paradoxical, was to say that what he had lost for ever was nothing. "Forever is a word that stretches backward too," he explained to himself. If any proof were needed his own behaviour was supplying it. He had ceased to believe in God but this was making no difference to him. Consequently what he had ceased to believe in had never been.

He sighed—the loud horse's sigh of one who has come to the end of a long stint. Then he stood up amid the rain and the ashes and stretched himself. He had got pins and needles in his legs from sitting still for so long, but it was a pleasure to his body to stretch and he stretched once more. The air struck cold on the muscles and skin which had, as it were, started to live again. He felt at once both tired and vigorous. In an odd way he was feeling rather pleased with himself, a pleasure that was perhaps the independent pleasure of his flesh which had waited patiently around his motionless thinking as a dog waits at the feet of its master absorbed in writing. The pen is thrown down rather wantonly, so that the ink may give a little spurt on to the page that a moment ago was all the world, that now is finished and prostrate and floutable. The master gets up and stretches, the dog gambols round him with congratulations. "Now you have come home to your senses again, now we can be reasonable and go for a walk!"

143

He leant down and gave Lueli a little shake, affectionate but brisk.

"Wake up, wake up. We are going down to the village now to find a lodging. You cannot sleep here in the rain all day or you will get rheumatism."

A policeman could not have been kinder, a mother more competent. He had got Lueli up and walking through the wet woods and eating stirabout by Ori's fire before he had had time to bethink him of his unhappiness.

Lueli sat swallowing and blinking and looking very debauched and youthful while Mr. Fortune and Ori made arrangements. For the present they could live under the chief's ample roof. Meanwhile the burnt hut could be rebuilt, or some dwelling could be fitted up to receive them as lodgers, whichever Mr. Fortune thought best. As for the volcano, that would not interfere with anybody's plans. The pigs had been corralled once more, the earthquake was already half-forgotten. Ori had sent an old woman up to the mountain to make a reconnaissance, and she had reported that the lava was flowing down the south side of the mountain where nobody lived. Everything was all right again, and the rain would freshen things

144

up nicely. To-morrow he would invite a few friends in, and there would be roast meat and a party in honour of his guest.

Personally Mr. Fortune would have preferred to have the former hut re-built and to go on living there, much as of old except for religion, the harmonium, and other European amenities. But he feared that Lueli would mope and be miserable. It would be better for him to have a change of scene, company and gaiety. Accordingly, he arranged that for the future they should lodge with Teioa, a lesser chief, whose family included several lively sons and daughters, and an extremely vivacious great-grandmother.

Unfortunately this plan worked badly. Mr. Fortune was much happier than he expected to be. He was now engaged in growing a beard, and freed from any obligation to convert his housemates he found their society very agreeable. The great-grandmother was especially good company. She was a celebrated story-teller, and when she had exhausted her stock of scandals about everyone in the village she fell back upon legends and fairy-tales. Mr. Fortune was interested to find that many of these were almost word for word the stories of the Old

Testament. One hot afternoon as they sat bathing their legs in a pool and waving away the flies from each other, she recounted the story of Joseph and his Brethren. Joseph was called Kila and was carried to the land of Egypt in a canoe, but all the familiar characters were there, all the familiar incidents, even to where Kila turned away from the brothers he was threatening, to hide the tears which he could no longer keep back. The only variation was in the character of Isaac, who had changed his sex and split into Joseph's mother and aunt. But in truth the change made little difference, nor did it detract from the dignity of the story, for in spite of our English prejudice there is nothing inherently ridiculous about a mother's sister. Mr. Fortune was not perturbed to hear the history of the Jews from the lips of a wrinkled and engraved old Polynesian harridan. He reflected that everywhere mankind is subject to the same anxious burden of love and loneliness, and must in self-defence enchant their cares into a story and a dream. In return for Joseph and his Brethren he told the old dame of the adventures of Mr. Pickwick, many of which were new to her.

But while Mr. Fortune was getting on so

nicely Lueli was very unhappy. His playmates had soon found out his misfortune. They teased him, saying that he had lost his god and would soon go to Hell. Every day the boy grew more dispirited. He shunned his fellows and went slinking off to hide himself in the woods, where he could mope in peace and quiet. Late in the evening he would creep back, smelling of damp forest earth and wild spices; and without a word he would lie down on his mat and fall into a dreary slumber.

One day Teioa remarked to Mr. Fortune: "That boy has lost his god. I expect he will die soon."

"What nonsense!" shouted Mr. Fortune in a loud rude voice. He felt too suddenly sick to choose his words. He remembered what he had once read in a book about the Polynesians: that they can renounce life at their own will, not with the splash of suicide but slowly, sullenly, deliberately, driving death into themselves like a wedge. Was Lueli doing this—gay, inconsequent, casual Lueli? But since the loss of his god Lueli was gay no longer, and his casualness had taken on a new and terrible aspect, as though it were the casualness of one who could not be bothered to live, who was discarding life as

147

naturally and callously as he had picked flowers and thrown them down to die.

Just then a troop of boys and girls danced by. They were dancing after Lueli and pelting him with small glittering fishes. "Catch!" they cried, "Here's a god for you, Lueli. Catch him!"

Lueli walked on as if he hadn't noticed them. He looked down and saw one of the fish lying at his feet. Like an animal he picked it up and began eating it, but he ate inattentively, without appetite. He was like a sick dog that snatches listlessly at a tuft of grass. Mr. Fortune stepped out from the verandah. His intention had been to drive the dancers away, but instead of that he put his arm through Lueli's and began walking him down to the beach.

"Let us bathe together," he said. "It is a long time since you gave me a swimming lesson."

Lueli swam so beautifully that it was hard to believe he was not happy. Mr. Fortune surpassed himself in flounderings. He tried to catch a fish in his mouth.

When they were sitting on the beach again he said: "Where shall we live when we leave

Teioa's house? Shall we make a new hut or shall we build up our old one again?"

"Go back to the old," Lueli replied instantly in a soft fearful whisper.

"Yes, I think so too. Our own bathing-pool is much the best."

"Yes. It's deeper than the one here."

"I think the fish are tamer, too."

"Yes."

"I was wondering if we couldn't make a small wickerwork bower on a pole and teach the parrots to sleep in it. In England people do so, only the birds are doves, not parrots. Perhaps you remember me telling you about our doves and pigeons?"

"They take messages."

"Yes, those are carrier pigeons. There are also pouters and fantails and tumbling pigeons that turn head over heels in the air. But parrots would be very nice too. You could feed them."

"Won't they be able to feed themselves?"

"Oh, yes, certainly. But they would be more apt to stay with us if we fed them."

"Must they stay?"

"Now am I diverting him from his grief"— thought Mr. Fortune, "or am I only boring him?"

149

The new hut that rose on the place of the old had a faint whiff of burning. Mr. Fortune had superintended the building of it and because the islanders were fond of him they allowed him to introduce several novelties, such as window-boxes and a kitchen dresser. He also threw out a bay. The parrot-cote stood in a corner of the lawn and leading up to it was a narrow ser-pentining path with crazy paving made out of flat shells. On the other side of the house to balance the parrot-cote was a pergola, con-structed in bamboo. In front of the house, in fact exactly where it always had been, but up-rooted by the earthquake, was the flat stone on which he had celebrated Holy Communion on that first Sunday morning. He looked at it a little sadly. He bore it no malice, although it reminded him of a special kind of happiness which he could taste no more. He decided that he would make it the head-stone of a rock-garden.

Mr. Fortune attached special importance to these European refinements because he felt that to the eyes of the world he must now present such an un-European appearance. The earth-quake had left him nothing save the clothes he stood up in, the contents of his pockets and a good-sized rubbish-heap. As for the rubbish-heap, he had with his own hands grubbed a large hole among the bushes and buried therein the bones of the harmonium, lamp, sewing-machine, etc., also the molten images of the communion plate and the tea-pot. He had done this by night, working by moonlight in the approved fashion of those who have a past to put away, and when he had covered in the hole and stamped down the earth he went back and forth from the ruins to the bushes, scooping up the ashes in a gourd and scattering them in the undergrowth.

His clothes he had folded and put away, thinking that as they were all he had, he had better save them up for future emergencies, such as a shipwreck, a visit of American tourists, the arrival of a new missionary or somebody dropping in from a flying-machine. In their stead he wore a kilt and a mantle of native cloth, soberly contrived without any fringes or fandangos, and sandals of plaited bark. Since this new garb was pocketless, the contents of his pockets were ranged on the shelf of honour of the kitchen dresser—a pocket magnifying-glass, a whistle, a nail-file, a graduated medicine spoon, a flint-and-steel lighter, a copper

medal commemorating Parnell which Henry
Martin had brought from Ireland as a curiosity,
nineteen mother-of-pearl counters in a wash-
leather bag, a pencil-sharpener blunted by sand
getting into it, a tape-measure that sprang back
into a boxwood nut, several buttons, a silver
pencil-case with no pencil and a small magnet,
painted scarlet. There was also the knife with
two blades, but this he carried on a string round
his neck.

He looked on this array without sentiment.
The parrot-cote and the pergola were also
without charms for him. His intentions were
severely practical. These things were all part of
his designs on Lueli, they were so many fish-
hooks to draw him from despair. Not by their
proper qualities, of course, Mr. Fortune was not
so simple as to expect that, even of the magnet.
But indirectly they would build up around their
owner and designer a compelling spiritual splen-
dour, a glamour of mysterious attributes, fas-
tidious living and foreign parts. After three
years of such familiarity it would not be easy
to re-construct his first fascination as something rich and strange. But it must be done if he
were to compete successfully with his rival in

Lueli's affections. It must be done because that rival was death.

He thought as little as he could help about his progress in this contest. He dared not allow himself to be elated when he seemed to be gaining a little, he dared not admit the possibility of failure. He fought with his eyes turned away from the face of the adversary, like Perseus attacking the Gorgon. He fought by inches, by half-hours; he dared not attempt a decisive victory for he could not risk a decisive defeat. And when he crept out of the hut at night to refresh himself with solitude and darkness, the sullen red light kindling and wavering above the blackness of the crags betokened to him that his enemy was also awake and weaving his powerful spells of annihilation.

He had no time to think of his own loss. He was entirely taken up with solicitude for Lueli, a soul no longer—as he supposed—immortal, and for that reason a charge upon him all the more urgent, as one is more concerned for a humming-bird than for a tortoise. Only at such times as when he had received a serious set-back or was feeling especially desperate did he find himself on the point of taking refuge in prayer;

and then remembering the real state of things he would feel exactly like a person who makes to cast himself down on a chair but recalls just in time (or maybe just too late) how all the furniture has been moved, and that the chair is no longer in its old place.

It was sometimes hard for him with his English prejudices not to grow irritated at Lueli's abject listlessness and misery. He could not have believed that his friend could be so chicken-hearted. And since when one is down everything falls on one, circumstances seemed to conspire in twitting and outraging the luckless youth.

Mr. Fortune thought he would try games. Lueli was agile and dexterous, surely it would comfort him to exhibit those qualities? Mr. Fortune introduced him to ping-pong. They played with basket-work bats and small nuts. On the second day a nut hit Lueli and made his nose bleed. He turned green, cast down his bat and began to whimper.

Since ping-pong was too rough, what about spellikins? He carved a set of pieces out of splinters, dyed them with fruit juice to make them look more appetising, and made a great show of excitement to tempt the other on.

Whenever it was Lueli's turn to hook a piece from the tangle he sighed and groaned as though he had been requested to move mountains. Dicing and skittles were no better received.

Deciding that neither games nor gaming (they diced for the mother-of-pearl counters) were likely to rouse Lueli from his dejection, Mr. Fortune cast about for some new expedient. Perhaps a pet animal might have charms? He caught a baby flying-fox and reared it with great tenderness on guavas and coco-milk. The flying-fox soon grew extremely attached to him and learnt to put its head out of the cage when he called "Tibby!" But whenever Lueli could be induced to take any interest in it and to prod it up with a cautious finger, it scratched and bit him. Still persevering with natural history, Mr. Fortune spat on the magnifying glass, polished it, and began to show off the wonderful details of flowers, mosses, and water-fleas. Lueli would look, and look away again, obediently and haplessly bored.

Though the idea of such cold and rapacious blood-thirstiness was highly repugnant to him, he resolved to sacrifice his own feelings (and theirs) and make a moth collection. He prepared a mess of honey and water and took Lueli out that evening on an expedition to lime the trees. Two hours later they went out again with a string of candle-nuts for a lantern and collected a quantity of moths and nocturnal insects, poignantly beautiful and battered with their struggles to escape. But he stifled his sense of shame, all the more in that Lueli seemed inclined to rise to this lure, of his own accord suggesting a second expedition. He had not quite grasped the theory, however. Two days later Mr. Fortune, returning from an errand in the village, was surprised to hear a loud and furious buzzing proceeding from the dell. It was full of wild bees, and Lueli, very swollen and terrified, came crawling out of the bushes. He had smeared the parrot-cote and the posts of the verandah with honey and it seemed as though every bee and wasp on the island were assembled together to quarrel and gorge themselves. It was not possible to approach the hut until after nightfall, and drunk and disorderly bees hovered about it for days, not to speak of a sediment of ants.

Worse was to come. Since his arrival on the island Mr. Fortune had never ailed. But now, whether by exposure to night dews and getting

his feet damp out mothing or by some special
malignity of Fate, he found himself feeling
sore at the back of the throat and sneezing; and
presently he had developed a streaming cold.
Lueli caught it from him and if his cold were
bad, Lueli's was ten times worse. He made no
effort to struggle against it; indeed, he was so
overwhelmed that struggling was practically
out of the question. He crouched on his mats,
snorting and groaning, with a face all chapped
and bloated, blear eyes, a hanging jaw, and a
sullen and unhealthy appetite; and every five
minutes or so he sneezed as though he would
bring the roof down.

Mr. Fortune was terrified, not only for
Lueli, but for the whole population of the island. He knew how direly European diseases
can rampage through a new field. He set up a
rigid quarantine. Since the loss of his God Lueli
had been at pains to avoid his friends, but
naturally he was now seized with a passionate
craving for their society; and there was some excuse for him as Mr. Fortune was not just now
very exhilarating company. But he did his best
to be, in spite of an ear-ache which followed
the cold, and between Lueli's paroxysms of
sneezing he strove to cheer him with accounts of

157

the Great Plague and the Brave Men of Eyam.

At last they were both recovered. But though restored in body Lueli was as mopish as ever. Mr. Fortune went on bracing, and beat his brains for some new distraction. But he had lost ground in this last encounter, and the utmost he could congratulate himself upon was that Lueli was still, however indifferently or unwillingly, consenting to exist. The worst of it was that he couldn't allow himself to show any sympathy. There were times when he could scarcely hold himself back from pity and condolence. But he believed that if he were once to acknowledge the other's grief he would lose his greatest hold over him—his title of being someone superior, august and exemplary.

And then one morning when they had been living in the new hut for about six weeks he woke up inspired. Why had he wasted so much time displaying his most trivial and uncompelling charms, opposing to the magnetism of death such fripperies and titbits of this world, such gewgaws of civilization as a path serpentining to a parrot-cote (a parrot-cote which hadn't even allured the parrots), or a pocket magnifying glass, while all the time he carried within him the inestimable treasures of intellectual enjoyment? Now he would pipe Lueli a tune worth dancing to, now he would open for him a new world. He would teach him mathematics.

He sprang up from bed, full of enthusiasm. At the thought of all those stretches of white beach he was like a bridegroom. There they were, hard and smooth from the tread of the sea, waiting for that noble consummation of blank surfaces, to show forth a truth; waiting, in this particular instance, to show forth the elements of plane geometry.

At breakfast Mr. Fortune was so glorified and gay that Lueli caught a reflection of his high spirits and began to look more life-like than he had done for weeks. On their way down to the beach they met a party of islanders who were off on a picnic. Mr. Fortune with delight heard Lueli answering their greetings with something like his former sociability, and even plucking up heart enough for a repartee. His delight gave a momentary stagger when Lueli decided to go a-picnicing too. But, after all, it didn't matter a pin. The beach would be as smooth again to-morrow, the air as sweet and nimble; Lueli would be in better trim for learning after a spree, and, now he came to think of it, he himself wouldn't teach any the worse for a little private rubbing-up beforehand.

It must be going on for forty years since he had done any mathematics; for he had gone into the Bank the same year that his father died, leaving Rugby at seventeen because, in the state that things were then in, the Bank was too good an opening to be missed. He had once got a prize—The Poetical Works of Longfellow —for Algebra, and he had scrambled along well enough in other branches of mathematics; but he had not learnt with any particular thrill or realized that thrill there might be until he was in the Bank, and learning a thing of the past.

Then, perhaps because of that never-ending entering and adding up and striking balances, and turning on to the next page to enter, add up and strike balances again, a mental occupation minute, immediate and yet, so to speak, wool-gathering, as he imagined knitting to be, the absolute quality of mathematics began to take on for him an inexpressibly romantic air. "Pure Mathematics." He used to speak of them to his fellow clerks as though he were hinting at some kind of transcendental debauchery of which he had been made free—and indeed there does seem to be a kind of unnatural vice in being so completely pure. After a spell of this holy boasting he would grow a little uneasy; and going to the Free Library he took out mathematical treatises, just to make sure that he could follow step by step as well as soar. For twenty pages perhaps, he read slowly, carefully, dutifully, with pauses for self-examination and working out the examples. Then, just as it was working up and the pauses should have been more scrupulous than ever, a kind of swoon and ecstasy would fall on him, and he read ravening on, sitting up till dawn to finish the book, as though it were a novel. After that his passion was stayed; the book went back to the Library and he was done with mathematics till the next bout. Not much remained with him after these orgies, but something remained: a sensation in the mind, a worshipping acknowledgment of something isolated and unassailable, or a remembered mental joy at the rightness of thoughts coming together to a conclusion, accurate thoughts, thoughts in just intonation, coming together like unaccompanied voices coming to a close.

But often his pleasure flowered from quite simple things that any fool could grasp. For instance he would look out of the bank windows, which had green shades in their lower halves; and rising above the green shades he would see a row of triangles, equilateral, isosceles, acute-angled, right-angled, obtuse-angled. These triangles were a range of dazzling mountain peaks, eternally snowy, eternally untrodden; and he could feel the keen wind which blew from their summits. Yet they were also a row of triangles, equilateral, isosceles, acute-angled, right-angled, obtuse-angled.

This was the sort of thing he designed for Lueli's comfort. Geometry would be much better than algebra, though he had not the same certificate from Longfellow for teaching it. Algebra is always dancing over the pit of the unknown, and he had no wish to direct Lueli's thoughts to that quarter. Geometry would be best to begin with, plain plane geometry, immutably plane. Surely if anything could minister to the mind diseased it would be the steadfast contemplation of a right angle, an existence that no mist of human tears could blur, no blow of fate deflect.

Walking up and down the beach, admiring

the surface which to-morrow with so much epiphany and glory was going to reveal the first axioms of Euclid, Mr. Fortune began to think of himself as possessing an universal elixir and charm. A wave of missionary ardour swept him along and he seemed to view, not Lueli only, but all the islanders rejoicing in this new dispensation. There was beach-board enough for all and to spare. The picture grew in his mind's eye, somewhat indebted to Raphael's Cartoon of the School of Athens. Here a group bent over an equation, there they pointed out to each other with admiration that the square on the hypotenuse equalled the sum of the squares on the sides containing the right angle; here was one delighting in a rhomboid and another in conic sections, that enraptured figure had secured the twelfth root of two, while the children might be filling up the foreground with a little long division.

By the morrow he had slept off most of his fervour. Calm, methodical, with a mind prepared for the onset, he guided Lueli down to the beach and with a stick prodded a small hole in it.

"What is this?"

"A hole."

"No, Lueli, it may seem like a hole, but it is a point."

Perhaps he had prodded a little too emphatically. Lueli's mistake was quite natural. Anyhow, there were bound to be a few misunderstandings at the start.

He took out his pocket knife and whittled the end of the stick. Then he tried again.

"What is this?"

"A smaller hole."

"Point," said Mr. Fortune suggestively.

"Yes, I mean a smaller point."

"No, not quite. It is a point, but it is not smaller. Holes may be of different sizes, but no point is larger or smaller than another point."

Lueli looked from the first point to the second. He seemed to be about to speak, but to think better of it. He removed his gaze to the sea.

Meanwhile, Mr. Fortune had moved about, prodding more points. It was rather awkward that he should have to walk on the beach-board, for his footmarks distracted the eye from the demonstration.

"Look, Lueli!"

164

Lueli turned his gaze inland.

"Where?" said he.

"At all these. Here; and here; and here. But don't tread on them."

Lueli stepped back hastily. When he was well out of the danger-zone he stood looking at Mr. Fortune with geat attention and some uneasiness.

"These are all points."

Lueli recoiled a step further. Standing on one leg he furtively inspected the sole of his foot.

"As you see, Lueli, these points are in different places. This one is to the west of that and consequently that one is to the east of this. Here is one to the south. Here are two close together, and there is one quite apart from all the others. Now look at them, remember what I have said, think carefully and tell me what you think."

Inclining his head and screwing up his eyes Lueli inspected the demonstration with an air of painstaking connoisseurship. At length he ventured the opinion that the hole lying apart from the others was perhaps the neatest. But if Mr. Fortune would give him the knife he would whittle the stick even finer.

"Now what did I tell you? Have you forgotten that points cannot be larger or smaller?

If they were holes it would be a different matter. But these are points. Will you remember that?"

Lueli nodded. He parted his lips, he was about to ask a question. Mr. Fortune went on hastily.

"Now suppose I were to cover the whole beach with these: what then?"

A look of dismay came over Lueli's countenance. Mr. Fortune withdrew the hypothesis.

"I don't intend to. I only ask you to imagine what it would be like if I did."

The look of dismay deepened.

"They would all be points," said Mr. Fortune, impressively. "All in different places. And none larger or smaller than another.

"What I have explained to you is summed up in the axiom: a point has position but not magnitude. In other words if a given point were not in a given place it would not be there at all."

Whilst allowing time for this to sink in he began to muse about those other words. Were they quite what he meant? Did they indeed mean anything? Perhaps it would have been better not to try to supplement Euclid. He turned to his pupil. The last words had sunk in at any rate, had been received without scruple and acted upon. Lueli was out of sight.

Compared with his intentions actuality had been a little quelling. It became more quelling as time went on. Lueli did not again remove himself without leave; he soon discovered that Mr. Fortune was extremely in earnest, and was resigned to regular instruction every morning and a good deal of rubbing-in and evocation during the rest of the day. No one ever had a finer capacity for listening than he, or a more docile and obliging temperament. But whereas in the old days these good gifts had flowed from him spontaneously and pleasurably he now seemed to be exhibiting them by rote and in a manner almost desperate, as though he were listening and obliging as a circus animal does its tricks. Humane visitors to circuses often point out with what alacrity the beasts run into the ring to perform their turn. They do not understand that in the choice of two evils most animals would rather flourish round a spacious ring than be shut up in a cage. The activity and the task is a distraction from their unnatural lot, and they tear through paper hoops all the better because so much of their time is spent behind iron bars.

167

It had been a very different affair when Lueli was learning Bible history and the Church Catechism, *The King of Love my Shepherd is* and *The Old Hundredth.* Then there had been no call for this blatant submission; lessons had been an easy-going conversation, with Lueli keeping his end up as an intelligent pupil should and Mr. Fortune feeling like a cross between wise old Chiron and good Mr. Barlow. Now they were a succession of harangues, and rather strained harangues to boot. Theology, Mr. Fortune found, is a more accommodating subject than mathematics; its technique of exposition allows greater latitude. For instance when you are gravelled for matter there is always the moral to fall back upon. Comparisons too may be drawn, leading cases cited, types and antetypes analysed and anecdotes introduced. Except for Archimedes mathematics is singularly naked of anecdotes.

Not that he thought any the worse of it for this. On the contrary he compared its austere and integral beauty to theology decked out in her flaunting charms and wielding all her bribes and spiritual bonuses; and like Dante at the rebuke of Beatrice he blushed that he should ever have followed aught but the noblest. No,

168

there was nothing lacking in mathematics. The deficiency was in him. He added line to line, precept to precept; he exhausted himself and his pupil by hours of demonstration and exposition; leagues of sand were scarred, and smoothed again by the tide, and scarred afresh: never an answering spark rewarded him. He might as well have made the sands into a rope-walk.

Sometimes he thought that he was taxing Lueli too heavily, and desisted. But if he desisted for pity's sake, pity soon drove him to work again, for if it were bad to see Lueli sighing over the properties of parallel lines, it was worse to see him moping and pining for his god. Teioa's words, uttered so matter-of-factly, haunted his mind. "I expect he will die soon." Mr. Fortune was thinking so too. Lueli grew steadily more lacklustre, his eyes were dull, his voice was flat; he appeared to be retreating behind a film that thickened and toughened and would soon obliterate him.

"If only, if only I could teach him to enjoy an abstract notion! If he could once grasp how it all hangs together, and is everlasting and harmonious, he would be saved. Nothing else can save him, nothing that I or his fellows can offer him. For it must be new to excite him and it

169

must be true to hold him, and what else is there that is both new and true?"

There were women, of course, a race of beings neither new nor true, yet much vaunted by some as a cure for melancholy and a tether for the soul. Mr. Fortune would have cheerfully procured a damsel (not that they were likely to need much of that), dressed her hair, hung the whistle and the Parnell medal round her neck, dowered her with the nineteen counters and the tape measure and settled her in Lueli's bed if he had supposed that this would avail. But he feared that Lueli was past the comfort of women, and in any case that sort of thing is best arranged by the parties concerned.

So he resorted to geometry again, and once more Lueli was hurling himself with frantic docility through the paper hoops. It was really rather astonishing, how dense he could be! Once out of twenty, perhaps, he would make the right answer. Mr. Fortune, too anxious to be lightly elated, would probe a little into his reasons for making it. Either they were the wrong reasons or he had no reasons at all. Mr. Fortune was often horribly tempted to let a mistake pass. He was not impatient: he was far more patient than in the palmiest days of theology—but he found

it almost unendurable to be for ever saying
with various inflexions of kindness: "No, Lueli.
Try again," or: "Well, no, not exactly," or:
"I fear you have not quite understood," or:
"Let me try to make that clearer." He withstood
the temptation. His easy acceptance (though in
good faith) of a sham had brought them to
this pass, and tenderness over a false currency
was not likely to help them out of it. No, he
would not be caught that way twice. Similarly
he pruned and repressed Lueli's talent for leak-
ing away down side-issues, though this was hard
too, for it involved snubbing him almost every
time he spoke on his own initiative.

Just as he had been so mistaken about the
nature of points, confounding them with holes
and agitating himself at the prospect of a beach
pitted all over, Lueli contrived to apply the
same sort of well-meaning misconceptions to
every stage of his progress—if progress be the
word to apply to one who is hauled along in a
state of semiconsciousness by the scruff of his
neck. When the points seemed to be tolerably
well-established in his mind Mr. Fortune led
him on to lines, and by joining up points he
illustrated such simple figures as the square, the
triangle and the parallelogram. Lueli perked up,

seemed interested, borrowed the stick and began joining up points too. At first he copied Mr. Fortune, glancing up after each stroke to see if it had been properly directed. Then growing rather more confident, and pleased—as who is not?—with the act of drawing on sand, he launched out into a more complicated design.

"This is a man," he said.

Mr. Fortune was compelled to reply coldly:

"A man is not a geometrical figure."

At length Mr. Fortune decided that he had better take in sail. Pure mathematics were obviously beyond Lueli; perhaps applied mathematics would work better. Mr. Fortune, as it happened, had never applied any, but he knew that other people did so, and though he considered it a rather lower line of business he was prepared to try it.

"If I were to ask you to find out the height of that tree, how would you set about it?"

Lueli replied with disconcerting readiness:

"I should climb up to the top and let down a string."

"But suppose you couldn't climb up it?"

"Then I should cut it down."

"That would be very wasteful: and the other

way might be dangerous. I can show you a better plan than either of those."

The first thing was to select a tree, an upright tree, because in all elementary demonstrations it is best to keep things as clear as possible. He would never have credited the rarity of upright trees had he not been pressed to find one. Coco-palms, of course, were hopeless: they all had a curve or a list. At length he remembered a tree near the bathing-pool, a perfect specimen of everything a tree should be, tall, straight as a die, growing by itself; set apart, as it were, for purposes of demonstration.

He marched Lueli thither, and when he saw him rambling towards the pool he recalled him with a cough.

"Now I will show you how to discover the height of that tree. Attend. You will find it very interesting. The first thing to do is to lie down."

Mr. Fortune lay down on his back and Lueli followed his example.

Many people find that they can think more clearly in a recumbent position. Mr. Fortune found it so too. No sooner was he on his back than he remembered that he had no measuring-stick. But the sun was delicious and the grass soft; he might well spare a few minutes in exposing the theory.

"It is all a question of measurements. Now my height is six foot two inches, but for the sake of argument we will assume it to be six foot exactly. The distance from my eye to the base of the tree is so far an unknown quantity. My six feet however are already known to you."

Now Lueli had sat up, and was looking him up and down with an intense and curious scrutiny, as though he were something utterly unfamiliar. This was confusing, it made him lose the thread of his explanation. He felt a little uncertain as to how it should proceed.

Long ago on dark January mornings, when a septic thumb (bestowed on him by a cat which he had rescued from a fierce poodle) obliged him to stay away from the Bank, he had observed young men with woollen comforters and raw-looking wind-bitten hands practising surveying under the snarling elms and whimpering poplars of Finsbury Park. They had tapes and tripods, and the girls in charge of perambulators dawdled on the asphalt paths to watch their proceedings. It was odd how vividly fragments of his old life had been coming back to him during these last few months.

He resumed:

"In order to ascertain the height of the tree I must be in such a position that the top of the tree is exactly in a line with the top of a measuring-stick—or any straight object would do, such as an umbrella—which I shall secure in an upright position between my feet. Knowing then that the ratio that height of the tree bears to the length of the measuring stick must equal the ratio that the distance from my eye to the base of the tree bears to my height, and knowing (or being able to find out) my height, the length of the measuring stick and the distance from my eye to the base of the tree, I can, therefore, calculate the height of the tree."

"What is an umbrella?"

Again the past flowed back, insurgent and actual. He was at the Oval, and out of an over-charged sky it had begun to rain again. In a moment the insignificant tapestry of lightish faces was exchanged for a noble pattern of domes, blackish, blueish and greenish domes, sprouting like a crop of miraculous and religious mushrooms. The rain fell harder and harder, presently the little white figures were gone from the field and, as with an abnegation of humanity, the green plain, so much smaller for their departure, lay empty and forsaken, ringed round with tier upon tier of blackly glistening umbrellas.

He longed to describe it all to Lueli, it seemed to him at the moment that he could talk with the tongues of angels about umbrellas. But this was a lesson in mathematics: applied mathematics, moreover, a compromise, so that all further compromises must be sternly nipped. Unbending to no red herrings he replied:

"An umbrella, Lueli, when in use resembles the—the shell that would be formed by rotating an arc of curve about its axis of symmetry, attached to a cylinder of small radius whose axis is the same as the axis of symmetry of the generating curve of the shell. When not in use it is properly an elongated cone, but it is more usually helicoidal in form."

Lueli made no answer. He lay down again, this time face downward.

Mr. Fortune continued: "An umbrella, however, is not essential. A stick will do just as well, so find me one, and we will go on to the actual measurement."

Lueli was very slow in finding a stick. He

looked for it rather languidly and stupidly, but Mr. Fortune tried to hope that this was because his mind was engaged on what he had just learnt.

Holding the stick between his feet, Mr. Fortune wriggled about on his back trying to get into the proper position. He knew he was making a fool of himself. The young men in Finsbury Park had never wriggled about on their backs. Obviously there must be some more dignified way of getting the top of the stick in line with the top of the tree and his eye, but just then it was not obvious to him. Lueli made it worse by standing about and looking miserably on. When he had placed himself properly he remembered that he had not measured the stick. It measured (he had had the forethought to bring the tape with him) three foot seven, very tiresome: those odd inches would only serve to make it seem harder to his pupil. So he broke it again, drove it into the ground, and wriggled on his stomach till his eye was in the right place, which was a slight improvement in method, at any rate. He then handed the tape to Lueli, and lay strictly motionless, admonishing and directing while Lueli did the measuring of the ground. In the interests of accuracy he did it thrice, each time with a different result. A few minutes before noon the height of the tree was discovered to be fifty-seven foot, nine inches.

Mr. Fortune now had leisure for compassion. He thought Lueli was looking hot and fagged, so he said:

"Why don't you have a bathe? It will freshen you up."

Lueli raised his head and looked at him with a long dubious look, as though he had heard the words but without understanding what they meant. Then he turned his eyes to the tree and looked at that. A sort of shadowy wrinkle, like the blurring on the surface of milk before it boils, crossed his face.

"Don't worry any more about that tree. If you hate all this so much we won't do any more of it, I will never speak of geometry again. Put it all out of your head and go and bathe."

Still Lueli looked at him as though he heard but didn't understand. Then in the same sleep-walking fashion he turned and went down to-wards the bathing-pool.

Presently, looking between the trees, Mr. Fortune saw him reappear on the rock above the deep part of the pool. He was going to dive. Very slowly and methodically he took off everything that was on him, he even took off his ear-rings. Then he stretched his arms in a curve above his head and leapt in.

A beautiful dive—Mr. Fortune found himself thinking of the arc of a stretched bow, the curve and flash of a scimitar, the jet of a harpoon—all instruments of death, all displaying the same austere and efficient kind of beauty, the swiftness to shed blood. A beautiful dive—and a long one. Had he come up already? Hardly; from where he sat Mr. Fortune could see almost the whole surface of the bathing-pool. Perhaps though he had come up behind the rock, swimming back under water.

Mr. Fortune rose to his feet. Instantly, with the movement, agonizing fear took hold of him. He ran down to the pool, and out along the rocks, shouting and calling. No sign, only the quietly-heaving water under the impervious blue sky. No sound, except the parrots and sea-birds, squawking in answer to his disturbing voice. Lueli was staying down on purpose. He was holding on to the sea-weed, drowning himself, with the resolute fatal despair of his light-hearted race.

Mr. Fortune leapt over his own fear of deep water. Where Lueli had dived, he could dive too. He hurled himself off the rock, he felt the water break like a stone under him, he felt himself smothered and sinking; and the next moment he was bouncing about on the surface, utterly and hopelessly afloat. He kicked and beat the water, trying to force a passage downward. It would not let him through.

He swam to the rock and scrambled out into the weight of air, and dived for a second time. Once more the sea caught him and held him up.

"Damn!" he said, softly and swiftly, as though he were pursuing a pencil which had rolled into a dark corner out of reach.

Since diving was out of the question he must run to the village to fetch helpers. The village was nearly a mile away, there might be no one there but old women and babies, he would be breathless, everyone would shout and wave their arms, by the time he got back with a rescue party it would be too late, Lueli would be drowned.

This time it was harder to haul himself out of the water, for he had forgotten to throw off his large draperies and they were now water-logged. After the shadow of the pool the sunlight seemed black and blinding. He started to run, loosening the knots as he went, for he would run quicker naked. As he threw off the cloak he caught sight over his shoulder of a canoe out to sea. It was heading away from the island but perhaps it was still within ear-shot. He shouted and waved the cloak and shouted and coo-eed again. Each cry came out of his body like a thing with jagged edges, tearing him inwardly. The canoe kept on its course. The sweat ran down and blinded him, so that he thought for a moment that the canoe had changed its direction and was coming to-wards him; but it was only the sweat in his eyes which had enlarged it.

He began to run again. It was a pity that he had wasted so much good breath shouting. He was among the trees now, rushing down a vista of light and shadow. Each tall tree seemed to gather speed as he approached it till it shot past him with a whirr of foliage and a swoop of darkness. His going shook the ground and the fruit fell off the bushes as he ran by.

The path began to wind downhill and grew stonier. He was about halfway to the village, he could hear the noise of the brook. He shot round a corner, tripped over something, and fell headlong into a group of human beings, falling among smooth brown limbs and cries of astonishment. It was one of those bevies, half-a-dozen young women who had come out to the brook to net crayfish. To his horror they all leapt to their feet and began to run away. Lying along the ground as he fell, with his head in the brook, he caught hold of an ankle.

"Stop! Don't be little fools!" he cried out, sobbing for breath. "Lueli is drowning in the bathing-pool. You must come back with me and save him."

The ankle belonged to Fuma, a hoyden whom he had once loathed beyond words; but now he adored her, for she was going to play up. She called back the other girls, rallied them, sent one back to the village, and bade the others run as fast as they could to the pool, and in a twinkling she and Mr. Fortune were following them up through the woods. Fuma caught hold of his arm and patted it encouragingly.

"He is in the deep hole under the black rock," he said. "He is lying there holding on to the weed. I have been shouting, and I may not be able to keep up with you. But you must run on without me and dive until you find him."

"Silly boy! Silly Lueli! He told me three days ago that he meant to die. Such nonsense!

Never mind, we will pull him up and breathe him alive again."

They ran on side by side. Presently Mr. Fortune said: "You know, Fuma, this is all my fault."

Fuma laughed ·ūnder her breath. "Lueli thinks the world of you," she said. "He is always telling us how lovable you are."

After a few more yards Mr. Fortune said: "Fuma, you must run on alone now."

She gave his arm a gentle nip, and shot ahead. He saw her join the others as a starling flies into the flock and then they were out of sight. He could only think of quite small immediate things, Fuma's eyebrows, a beautiful clear arch, and the soft quick sound of her breathing. He was thinking more of her than of Lueli. She seemed more real.

He was still running but now every time that he put a foot down it was with a stamp that disintegrated his balance, so that he could not guide his direction. Then he heard a splash, and another and another. They had reached the pool and begun diving. Then he heard Fuma's voice crying: "Further to the left. He's down here." Then a babble of voices and more splashings. Then silence.

He gathered up his will for the last thirty yards, was down on to the beach and out breast-high into the water. He saw a girl's head rise above the surface of the empty pool. She shook the hair from her eyes, saw him standing there, and came swimming towards him.

"We've got him," she said. "But Fuma has to cut the weed with a shell for we can't loosen his hands."

Mr. Fortune took the pocket-knife from his neck and held it out to her. Then he saw a strangely intricate and beautiful group emerge and slowly approach. They had brought up Lueli and were bearing him among them. His head lolled and dipped back into the water from Fuma's shoulder, where it lay. His eyes were open in a fixed and piteous stare, his mouth was open too, and a little trickle of blood ran down from his lip, where he had bitten it. His inanimate body trailed in the water with gestures inexpressibly weary. But two long streamers of weed still hung from his clenched hands.

Death comes with her black ruler and red ink and scores a firm line under the long tale of more or less, debit and credit, all the small multitudinous entries which have made up the relationship between one's self and another. The line is drawn, the time has come to audit; and from the heart of her shadow a strange clarity, dream-like and precise, is shed upon the page, so that without any doubt or uncertainty we can add up the account which is now at an end, and perceive the sum-total of the expenditure of time. While the others were ministering around the body of Lueli, squeezing the water out of his lungs, rubbing him, breathing into his nostrils, burning herbs and performing incantations, Mr. Fortune sat under a tree, a little apart, and audited the past. In the tree sat a parrot, uttering from time to time its curious airy whistle—a high, sweet, meditative note. It seemed to Mr. Fortune that the bird was watching the process of his thoughts, and that its whistle, detached from any personal emotion, even from that of astonishment, was an involuntary and philosophic acknowledgment of the oddity of men's lives and passions.

"I loved him," he thought. "From the moment I set eyes on him I loved him. Not with what is accounted a criminal love, for though I set my desire on him, it was a spiritual desire. I did not even love him as a father loves a son, for that is a familiar love, and at the times when Lueli most entranced me it was as a

being remote, intact, and incalculable. I waited
to see what his next movement would be, if he
would speak or no—it was the not knowing
what he would do that made him dear. Yes, that
was how I loved him best, those were my happi-
est moments: when I was just aware of him,
and sat with my senses awaiting him, not wishing to speak, not wishing to make him notice me
until he did so of his own accord because no
other way would it be perfect, would it be by
him. And how often, I wonder, have I let it be
just like that? Perhaps a dozen times, perhaps
twenty times all told, perhaps, when all is put
together, for an hour out of the three years I
have had with him. For man's will is a demon
that will not let him be. It leads him to the edge
of a clear pool; and while he sits admiring it,
with his soul suspended over it like a green
branch and dwelling in its own reflection, will
stretches out his hand and closes his fingers upon
a stone—a stone to throw into it.

"I'd had a poor meagre turnpike sort of life
until I came here and found Lueli. I loved
him, he was a refreshment to me, my only
pleasant surprise. He was perfect because he *was*
a surprise. I had done nothing to win him, he
was entirely gratuitous. I had had no hand in

him, I could no more have imagined him before hand than I could have imagined a new
kind of flower. So what did I do? I started in-
terfering. I made him a Christian, or thought I
did, I taught him to do this and not to do the
other, I checked him, I fidgetted over him. And
because I loved him so for what he was I could
not spend a day without trying to alter him.
How dreadful it is that because of our wills we
can never love anything without messing it
about! We couldn't even love a tree, not a stone
even; for sooner or later we should be pruning
the tree or chipping a bit off the stone. Yet if
it were not for a will I suppose we should cease
to exist. Anyhow it is in us and while we live
we cannot escape from it; so however we love
and whatever we love it can only be for a few
minutes, and to buy off our will for those few
minutes we have to relinquish to it for the rest
of our lives whatever it is we love. Lueli has
been the price of Lueli. I enslaved him, I kept
him on a string. I robbed him of his god twice
over—first in intention, then in fact. I made
his misery more miserable by my perpetual in-
terference. Up till an hour ago I was actually
tormenting him with that damned geometry.
And now he is dead. . . . Yes, parrot! You

187

may well whistle. But be careful. Don't attract
my attention too much lest I should make a pet
of you, and put you in a cage, and then in the
end, when you had learnt to talk like me instead of whistling like a wise bird, wring your
neck because you couldn't learn to repeat Para-
dise Lost."

At these words the parrot flew away, just as
though it had understood and wished to keep
on the safe side; and looking up Mr. Fortune
saw some of the islanders running towards him.
He got up and went to meet them. "Well, is
he dead?" he asked, too deeply sunk in his own
wan-hope to pay any attention to their looks and
greetings.

It was some time before they could make him
understand that Lueli was alive. He followed
them, dumb, trembling and stupefied, to where
Lueli was sitting propped up under a tree. He
looked rather battered, and rather bewildered,
and slightly ashamed of himself, like a child that
has been at a rich tea-party, grown over-
excited and been sick. But the hag-ridden look
he had worn since the earthquake was gone, and
he was answering the congratulations and chaff
of those around him with a semblance of his
old gaiety.

Mr. Fortune stood looking down on him in silence, confused at meeting him whom he had not thought to meet again. Lueli was infected by his embarrassment, and the two regarded each other with caution and constraint, as dear friends do who meet unexpectedly after long separation. Lueli was the first to speak.

"How ill you look. Your face is all holes."

"Lueli, you would have laughed if you could have seen me trying to dive in after you. Twice I threw myself in, but I could do nothing but float."

"I expect you let yourself crumple up."

"Yes, I expect I did."

"But it was very kind of you to try."

"Not at all."

The situation was horrible. Mr. Fortune was tongue-tied, very jealous of the others and haunted with the feeling that behind all this cause for rejoicing there was some fatal obstacle which he ought to know all about but which his mind was shirking the contemplation of. Lueli fidgetted and made faces. The awkwardness of being raised from the dead was too much even for his *savoir faire*.

"Why can't I be natural?" thought Mr. Fortune. "Why can't I say how glad I feel? And

189

why don't I feel my gladness? What have I done? Why is it like this, what is the matter with me?"

Lueli's thoughts were something like this: "He has a blemish on his neck, but didn't I ever notice it before? It must have grown larger. I hope they won't begin to laugh at him because he can't dive. I love him, but Oh dear! what a responsibility he is. I don't think I can bear it much longer, not just now. I don't want responsibilities. I only want to go to sleep."

Round them stood half the population of the island, raging with congratulations, jokes and enquiries. Even when they had escorted them back to the hut, superintended Lueli's falling asleep, and eaten all the provisions which Mr. Fortune brought out to them, they would not go away but sat among their crumbs and on the rock-garden imploring Fuma to tell them once more how Mr. Fortune had come bounding through the wood and fallen headlong into the girls' laps.

For no reason that he could see he had suddenly become immensely popular. And as he walked to and fro in the twilight waiting for his guests to take themselves off he heard his

name being bandied about in tones of the live-
liest affection and approval. He had one consolation: by the morrow he would be out of fashion again. As for Lueli, they scarcely mentioned
him. If he had been drowned they would
have spent the evening wailing and lamenting;
not for him but for themselves, at the reminder
of their own mortality, after the natural way
of mourning. And there would have been just
as much gusto, he thought—but tenderly, for
he felt no animosity to them now, only a desire
to get rid of them and be left to his own soul
—and just as many crumbs.

The moon had set before they went away.
Mr. Fortune stole into the hut and listened for
a while to Lueli's quiet breathing, a slight human rhythm recovered that day from the
rhythm of the sea. He knelt down very quietly
and creakingly and taking hold of Lueli's limp
warm hand he put it to his lips. "Good-bye, my
dear," he murmured under his breath. Lueli
stirred, and uttered a drowsy inarticulate Good-
night.

Both rhythms were in Mr. Fortune's ears as
he lay down to rest. He did not sleep, at least
not for some hours; but he lay unharried in a

solemn and dream-like repose, listening to the gentle fanning of Lueli's slumber and the slow tread of the sea.

Thus, tranquil and full of long thoughts, he had lain on his first night in Fanua, gazing at the star Canopus and watching the trail of creeper stir at the sweet breath of night. All that he had then of hope and faith was lost. But now at the last he seemed strangely to have resumed the temper of that night, and the thought of his renunciation was as full and perfect as the former thought of his vocation had been. "It is not one's beliefs that matter," he told himself, "but to be acting up to them. To have come to Fanua and now to have made up my mind to go away—it is the decision that fills me with this amazing kind of joy."

To go away. It was the only solution, he had the parrot's word for it. The slow tread of the sea told him the same story. "I brought you here," it said, "and presently I shall bear you away. My ebbing tides will return to Fanua, and ebb and return again and ebb and return again. But for you there will be no return." And the tread of the sea became the footfall of a warder. It was this necessity, still implicit and unrealized, which had lain like a stone in his heart when he saw Lueli brought back from the dead. If he had not thought of Lueli as being dead, he would never have understood. But Death had vouchsafed him a beam of her darkness to see clearly by; and having seen, he could not sin against that light. He must go away, that was the only stratagem by which love could outwit its own inherent treachery. If he stayed on, flattering himself with the belief that he had learnt his lesson, he would remember for a while no doubt; but sooner or later, inevitably he would yield to his will again, he would begin to meddle, he would seek to destroy.

To see everything so clearly and to know that his mind was made up was almost to be released from human bondage. This must be the boasted calm joy of mathematicians which he had once pretended to share. Euclid had failed him or he had failed Euclid; but the contemplation of his own reasoning and resolved mind gave him a felicity beyond even that which the rightness of right-angles could afford. He would keep awake a little longer and make the most of it. He could be sure it would not last. But when it had shattered and desolation came in its stead there would still be common-sense and common manliness and several practical preoccupations with which to keep desolation at bay.

First he must get a message to St. Fabien. In the pocket of the coat he had worn on the night of the earthquake were a couple of sheets torn out of an exercise book. He had carried them on his stroll on the chance that he might feel impelled to write a sonnet (Petrarchan Sonnets were the only poetical form he attempted because they were so regular, and even so he did them very badly) On The Setting Sun, or To a Hermit Crab. He had not done so, partly because he had forgotten to take a pencil too; but now, when he had smoothed the crumples out, these sheets would come in handy for his letter to the Archdeacon.

In the morning he gathered some purple fruit whose juice he knew from experience to be indelible, squeezed them into a bowl, and with a reed pen wrote as follows:

Fanua.

My dear Archdeacon.

I am sorry to trouble you but I must ask that the launch may be sent to fetch me away from Fanua. My ministry here has been a failure. I have converted no one, moreover I think that they are best as they are.

I am aware that I shall seem to you an unprofitable servant, and I am prepared for reproof. But I must tell you that in my present state of mind nothing that you can say, either of blame or consolation, is likely to make much difference.

I should be very much obliged if you could send with the launch a pair of stout black boots (size eleven) some collars (sixteen and a half inch), and a bottle of Aspirin tablets.

Yours sincerely,
TIMOTHY FORTUNE.

P.S. Also some bone collar-studs. There was an earthquake and I lost those which I had.

When the letter was written he put it away. His mind was quite made up as to leaving Fanua, there was no danger that a week's delay or so in sending off the letter would weaken his resolution. Indeed if he had consulted his own feelings he would not have delayed for an hour. But he did not wish to leave Lueli until he was quite certain the boy was able to stand on his own feet.

One thing was beyond doubt: Lueli would not try to kill himself again. He had been frightened by the dark look of Death under the water. Though he said nothing about his drowning or his rescue it was obvious that he had set himself to get on good terms with the life he had then thought fit to abandon. Never before had he been so beautiful, nor moved so lithely, nor sprawled so luxuriously on the warm grass. Sleek, languid and glittering, he was like a snake that has achieved its new skin. He was grown more sociable too, and with a quite new form of sociability; for instead of seeking the company of others he exerted himself to make others seek his. Although his drowning had done him no harm whatsoever and he had never been in better trim, he chose to preen himself as an interesting invalid. At all hours of the day the youth and beauty of the island would appear with offerings of fruit and invalid delicacies. Since the Fanuans are a people unequalled in kindness and idleness this was not such a great tribute to Lueli's fascinations. But what was really remarkable was the success with which he imposed himself upon them as a young hero. Even Fuma, who had stood out against his pretensions for several days, laughing at him and pulling his hair and making sarcastic remarks about people who couldn't swim, suddenly dropped her sisterly airs and attended on him as devoutly as the rest. As though this were the last plum that he had been proposing should drop into his mouth Lueli began to feel a little better now; was able to go sailing or swimming—not even the waters that drowned him could quench his love for water—or to take a stroll in the woods. Presently he was addressing Fuma as "Child."

If he had not so utterly forsworn meddling, if the letter to the Archdeacon were not put away in his coat pocket, Mr. Fortune might have yielded himself to a glow of match-making. Perhaps Fuma was not quite the girl he would have chosen; perhaps for that matter Lueli's choice of her was not quite to the exclusion of other girls; but having been so heart-rent over the defeated estate of that spiritless and godless boy whom even his own younger brothers had been able to tease out of the village it would have been sweet now to abet the happiness of this triumphant young man.

As things were Lueli's recovery must be the waving of the flag which signalled his departure. So one morning he set off to find Ori and explained to him that he wished to send a message by canoe to Maikalua. Would Ori as usual see about it and oblige?

Early in the morning the canoe was launched: and singing and shouting the boatmen set out on their voyage.

As he watched them depart Mr. Fortune had a sudden vision of a pillar-box. It seemed to spring up before him, a substantial scarlet cylinder, out of the glittering untenanted beach. He remembered how long ago, one August afternoon, he had posted a note accepting with pleasure an invitation to play tennis, an invitation which came from some people called Tubbs who lived at Ealing; and how having done so, he stood with the sun beating down upon him, just outside the station, with people jostling past him and the newspaper man shouting: "Star, Standard, Westminster! Surrey all out!" wishing with despair that he could get his note back, for it seemed to him that nothing could be more distasteful than to play tennis at Ealing with those rollicking Tubbses.

But now he had no wish to recall his letter, though he was still sick with the wrench of definitely despatching it. His only thought was to leave Fanua as soon as possible; and until the moment of departure came he could not imagine how he would pass away the time. Gradually the pillar-box faded out before him and he saw the ocean-waste, the narrow diminishing boat, the empty indifferent sky. His head was aching again and he put his hand to his forehead. There was that deluded watch, mincing complacently on. It was much better at passing away time than he. Half-past seven. Another thirteen hours and he would be getting himself supper, and Lueli might come in or he might not. And after supper he would be going to bed. But if he fell asleep too soon he would wake early with another shining unending morning before him. No! It would be better to sit up late, to midnight if possible. For time passes more tolerantly at night when the body is drowsy and the mind tired; but in the morning hours there is no release from one's faculties, and every second is a needleprick to consciousness.

The sand had dribbled out between his fingers, he found himself staring at the palm of his hand. It would be the better for washing; and he turned back toward the bathing pool. While he was still the headache was not so bad; but every step jolted it and sent a heavy sick tingle up his spine to jar against his temples.

As the bathing-pool came in sight through

the lattice of ferns and bushes he paused, for it came into his mind that Lueli might be there with his friends. And dropping on his hands and knees he crawled through the undergrowth, holding his breath and cautiously poking out his head from the greenery to scout if the coast were clear. He need not have been so discreet. The pool was empty. There was no foot-print on the sandy rim.

He undressed and bathed his body wearily in the fresh cool water—it was always exquisitely cool under the shadow of the rock. It did not occur to him that by going a little further he could drown. He hauled himself up on a ledge and began to clean his toes with a wisp of sea-weed.

The shade on his wet limbs, the sound of the sea, the breathing murmur of the woods in the soft steady wind was comforting to his headache. He began to feel slightly lachrymose and a good deal better, and with the tenderness of a convalescent he watched the fish darting in and out of the streaming weed. Of course he might have gone himself by the canoe instead of sending his request for the launch. But though he now realized that it would have been perfectly feasible to have done so, something within him assured him that it would not really have been possible. Things must take their course: and thus to wait still in Fanua for the launch to come and fetch him away was the natural course for his departure. He could see himself leaving the island in the launch, but not any other how.

That bull-faced fish had dodged in and out from the weed a dozen times at least. It was as persistent as a swallow. His body was dry now and his headache smoothed away. Only the heartache remained; and he was getting used to that.

All this while, as he was crawling through the bushes, and cleaning his toes, and watching the fish, there had been but one deep preoccupying thought at the back of his mind—the thought of Lueli and a longing for his presence. It was on the chance that Lueli might come down to bathe that he was waiting now. And he imagined the conversation that must take place between them.

"Lueli, I am going away from Fanua."

"But you will come back again?"

"No. I am going away for ever."

It would be quite simple—as simple as that. "I am going away from Fanua." Above all he was determined that there should be no explana-

tions. It would never do to tell Lueli that he
was going away because of him. No smirch of
complicity, no blight of responsibility should
fall upon Lueli, happy Lueli who had done him
no wrong, and whom so often he had sought to
injure from the best, worst, most fatal and
affectionate motives. How could he have so
teased him in his misery with that idiotic geometry—a misery, too, in which he was the agent,
for it was through him that Lueli had lost his
idol. That was bad enough, at any rate it was
damnably silly. Though what else could he
have done? Something equally senseless, no
doubt. But what was it to his behaviour in
the hut, when the idol lay between them, and
Lueli crouched in his last refuge of silence
while he sought with menaces and blackmailing
to rob him of his faith, and bade him cast his
god into the fire? Ah! of the two gods who
had perished that night it was the wooden one
he would now fetch back again.

But this he could never say. He must not
give any reason for his departure lest he should
at length fall into giving the true one and seeming to involve Lueli in his own blunders. "I
am going away from Fanua." That must be
all. Little to say: so little that he must postpone

saying it till the last hour came, the hour when one says Good-bye. And for that reason he must shun Lueli's presence, hide from him if need be and crawl through bushes, for if he once allowed himself to resume their old familiar intercourse he would not be able to keep back the words: "Lueli, I am going away. I am going away for ever."

He said it aloud, and as it were heard the words for the first time. He put on his clothes and began mechanically to walk back toward the hut. Then he had a good idea. Since he was leaving the island it would be a pity not to go up the mountain and have a look at the crater. Very likely he would never have another opportunity of inspecting an active volcano.

It would be a taxing expedition, and not without danger. He put up some food, cut himself a stout walking-stick and gathered a bunch of plantain leaves to stick in his boots—for it was decidedly an occasion for boots. Preparations always pleased him, for he had a house-wifely mind, and by the time he set out he was feeling, if not less miserable, at any rate a point or two deflected from his misery.

The new crater was on the further side of the mountain. He decided that the best way of approach would be to walk up through the woods by tracks which he knew and thence to skirt round under the foot of the crags, keeping against the wind in order to avoid the smoke and fumes. As he mounted through the woods he could hear, at first the sea and the tree-tops, presently the murmuring tree-tops alone. Soothed by their company and their shade he climbed on peacefully enough for a couple of hours, keeping a sharp look-out for rents and fissures; for however weary one may be of life one would not choose to discard it by starving, or suffocating in a deep crevice as hot as an oven.

At last he came out upon the tract of scrub and clinker which covered the upper slopes of the mountain. After the cool depth of the woodland it was like a pale hell, a prospect bleached and brittle, such as even the greenest garden will offer if one sits and looks at it suddenly after lying with the sun strong on one's eyelids. After a moment of dizziness the garden will revive again, but the longer Mr. Fortune looked at this landscape the more spectral and repellent it seemed. And because the air quivered with heat the face of the mountain-side seemed to be twitching with fear.

There were the crags, some two miles away yet, but looking as though he could throw a stone and splinter them. They were not rhododendron-coloured now, but a reddish and scabby mottle. They reminded him of a group of ruined gas-vats with the paint scaling off them, standing in the middle of a brick-field. It smelt of brick-fields too; and in the place of the former sounds of the sea and the tree-tops new sounds came to his ear, ugly to match the landscape, and of a kind of baleful insignificance like the landscape—far-off crashes and rumblings, the hiss and spurt of escaping steam: the noise of a flustered kitchen.

Now was the moment to put the plantain leaves in his boots. Those which he had gathered were faded, he threw them away and gathered fresh. Then, with a heart beating harshly and remotely, he set forth on the second stage of his climb.

It was hateful going—slippery bents, bristling scrubs, sharp-edged clinker which hurt his feet. He tripped and fell constantly, and when he fell the clinker cut his hands. Twice he remained crumpled on the ground just as he had fallen, gasping for breath, and cowed by the frantic beating of his heart, which did not seem to belong to him, behaving like some wild animal which, terrified and apprehensive, is dragged struggling to the summit of the mountain to be sacrificed there. And as he went on, the brickfield smell grew stronger, and the kitchen noises grew louder, and the sun striking down on him from the motionless sky, striking up at him from the ground, reverberating upon him from the parched landscape, enclosed him in its burning net.

He remembered the story of the woman Kapiolani, the Christian convert of Hawaii. Followed by a crowd of trembling islanders she had gone up the burning mountain to manifest her faith in the true God. When she was come to the crater of Kilauea she had scrambled down to the very edge of the burning lake, and there, half hidden in clouds of smoke, she called on Pele the Fire-goddess, and flouted her, calling her an impostor and challenging her, if goddess she were, to rise up out of her everlasting fiery den and overwhelm her accuser with its waves. Pele did not answer: she sulked in the heart of her fire, powerless before the name of Christ. And when she had waited long enough Kapiolani climbed up again out of the pit and showed herself once more to the crowd who had been cowering at the crater-side, trembling, and listening to the loud voice of her faith. And when they saw her, they believed.

Her faith, thought Mr. Fortune, had carried her lightly up the mountain-side, and over the lava-flow which she had trodden with scorched and bleeding feet. But he, though a man, and born free from the burden of heathen fears, and wearing boots, was already tired out and reluctant, and only a cold tourists' curiosity could carry him onward, and a bargain-hunting spirit which told him that having gone so far it would be a waste not to go on to the end.

Kapiolani had made her act of faith in the year 1825. And after that, as though for her courage she were like the prophetess Deborah, the land had peace thirty years. Then Pele shook herself contemptuously and fell to her tricks again. At her first shake the island trembled, as though it knew what was to come. "Yet a little," said the Fire-goddess; and slept for another ten years. This time she woke angrier. The island quivered like the lid of a boiling pot, a river of fire, flowing terribly underground, rent open a green and fertile plain, and five times a tidal wave reared up and fell upon the helpless land. And once more Pele fell asleep,

but fell asleep to dream; snarling to herself, and
hotly, voluptuously, obscurely triumphing in a
dream of what her next awakening would be.

Kapiolani would not know of that awakening at any rate. It was to be hoped that she had
been spared the others. A simple faith like hers
would be cruelly jolted by such ambiguities in
God's law. She might even have lost it thereby,
as did Voltaire, another blunt, straightforward
thinker, at a rather similar exhibition; for
she could hardly be expected to take the subtler
view of those long-standing and accustomed be-
lievers who can gloss over an eruption as a very
justifiable protest against the wickedness of their
neighbours. And as for saying that it is all a
mystery—well, there is not much satisfaction
to be got out of that.

These thoughts carried him over the last
mile, and looking up he was surprised to find
himself under the crags. He began to skirt
round them. Now the noises and the smells
were so strong that as he rounded every jut of
the crags he expected to come on the new crater. Just as he had climbed on to the top of a
large rock a gust of wind, veering among the
crags, brought with it a volley of foul smoke,

which rose up from beneath him and smothered him round, just as smoke comes suddenly
belching out of the vent of a tunnel. He stood
for a moment coughing and stifling; and then
the wind shifted again, and the smoke lifted
away from him, and looking out underneath
it he saw that he was come to the end of his
search.

The rock on which he stood was the last
westernmost redoubt of the crags, and before
him extended the other side of the island of
Fanua. Far off and strangely high up he saw
the sea-line. The ocean seemed to fall steeply
and smoothly downhill to where it broke upon
the reef in a motionless pattern of foam.
Stretching away down the mountain-side was a
long, serpentining slab of lava—the thickly-
burning torrent which had torn apart the flanks
of the mountain on the night of the eruption,
wallowing downward with an ever more heavy
and glutted motion until now it was solidifying
into rock; a brutal surface of formless hummocks and soppy and still-oozing fissures. Everything around was deep in ashes, and here and
there little gushes of steam showed where the
heat still worked under the outer crust. It was

like the surface of a saucepan of porridge which has been lifted off the fire but still pimples and undulates with its own heat.

Another jet of smoke belched up. Holding his breath Mr. Fortune crept over the rock on his hands and knees and looked down into the crater.

By night the spectacle might have had a sort of Medusa's head beauty, forever wakeful and writhing and dangerous; but in the light of day it was all sordid and despairing. Thick smoke hung low over the burning lava, and thin gaseous flames flickered on the surface, livid and cringing, like the ghosts of bad men still haunting around the corrupting body. Below the play of dun smoke and shadowy flame the lava moved unceasingly, impelled to the south, on and on and over and over as though its torment were bound upon an axle. Every now and then two currents would flow into each other with a heavy impact, a splash and a leap of fire. And then it was as though it clapped hands in its agony.

Slowly, because he was cramped with having watched it so long, Mr. Fortune raised himself to his feet and turned away. He had no thoughts, no feelings. What he had seen was

something older than the earth; but vestigial,
and to the horror of the sun what the lizard is
to the dragon: degenerate. Shuddering and cold
he went down past the shadow of the crags and
over the scorched expanse of hell-ground towards the woods, hastening, still having in his
ears the growlings and concussions of the pit
and with that foul smell still in his nostrils.

When he came into the woods he stopped
and looked up. The green boughs hid away the
skies. He was glad. He did not want to look
at anything eternal just now. He sat down on
a fallen tree. Moss covered it, and creepers
and tree-ferns were springing out of it; but he
parted the ferns and creeper and scratched away
the moss and put down his nose to snuff up the
scent of decay. Everywhere in the woods was
the odour of mortality; it was sweet to him,
like a home-coming. He lay down and buried
his face in the leaf-mould, pressing his eye-lids
to the warm mouldering softness, trying to forget the rock.

When he felt better he went on again; and
coming to a stream he bathed himself, and ate
some fruit. He was not very sure of his whereabouts, so to follow the stream seemed the best
plan. It was a pleasant guide. He heard it sing-

ing ahead as he followed its windings. All this part of the woodland was unknown to him. It seemed very venerable and solitary. The solemn girth and glossy great leaves of the breadfruit trees pleased him all the better because he was thinking of them as beings transient and subject to laws of growth and decay. They were steadfast, he thought, because they knew of their appointed end. They soothed him, bearing faithful witness that his own should be no other— that he too should one day lie along the earth and be gathered into it.

It occurred to him for the first time that now he would not, as he had hoped, be buried in Fanua. And as though the thought had called up a vision, he saw what appeared to be a graveyard before him. It was a sort of pound or enclosure, built of rough stones. Whatever the purpose of the place it was clearly unfrequented, perhaps forsaken; for the mossy walls were breached and tumbled and the grass grew clean and untrodden in the entry. Overhead the breadfruit trees mingled their large boughs like a roof of wings. He turned and went in. He found himself surrounded by ranks of idols, idols of all sizes and all fashions, idols of wood and stone, all very old, subdued with weather, moss-grown, with the grass tangling round their bases. He knew well what they must be: in this island where everyone had his own god these were the gods of the dead. At the death of their worshippers the gods were carried here and left to their repose, till they too in their time failed and sank into the earth. He remembered who had died since he came to the island and peered among the idols for some more recent than the others which might be those of his acquaintance. Yes, that was Akau's god perhaps, and that pot-bellied fellow with the humorous squint might be the god of poor old Live-for-Ever. Only Lueli's god would never come here.

Sad Lueli! Just now in his flourish of youth and affability he might forget his lost god and do quite as well without him; but one day Lueli would be growing old and then—then he would feel his loss. For the day must come when a man turns from the companionship of flesh and blood, be it flesh and blood failing like his own, or the flesh and blood he has begotten, and seeks back into the traditions of his race for a companionship more ghostly and congenial—old habits, old beliefs, old stories—the things his childhood accepted and his forefathers lived by. In that day Lueli would need his god. The lack of it would be a kind of disgrace, a mutilation.

"I cannot go from Fanua," said Mr. Fortune, standing among the idols: "until I have given Lueli back his god."

The knife hung round his neck: it would be easy to take one of the idols, re-trim its features, scrape off the moss and make a new idol of it. But a feeling of decorum stayed his hand. However, he might study them, for he would need an example. He spent half an hour or so in the enclosure, kneeling before the idols, examining the details of their workmanship and trying to acquire the convention. Then, for it was still afternoon, he spent some time wandering round in search of a suitable piece of wood. It must be about two foot long, straight, without knots, not so fresh as to tear, not so old as to crumble, of an easy grain to carve, and for choice, of a pleasant colour. He sought out several pieces and experimented on them with his knife before he found one to his liking. It was of rather dark, sweet-smelling wood, of what tree he knew not, for he found it lying beside the stream. A freshet must have carried it there, perhaps from the hands of some other woodman; for there seemed to be cutting-marks about one end of it.

He sat down and began to rough out the image he had in his mind: a man with a bird perched on his wrist, his head a little inclined towards the bird as though it were telling him something; and seated at his feet a plain smooth dog, also looking at the bird, but quite kindly. After so many failures, great and small: the trousers, the introduction to mathematics, all his very indifferent attempts at cookery, boiled bad eggs and clammy coco-nut buns, the conversion of the islanders and the domestication of the parrots, it might have been expected of Mr. Fortune that he would put forth on sculpture with diffidence. But his heart was in it; he had never attempted anything of the kind before; and anyhow, it is the vainglorious people who expect difficulties. Mr. Fortune in his modesty supposed that cookery, conversion, etc., were really quite easy matters, and that it was only he who made a botch of them. So when after an hour or so of whittling and measuring and whittling again, he found himself possessed of a considerable aptitude for wood-carving, and the man, the dog and the bird emerging from

215

the billet with every promise of looking very much as he intended them to, he was pleased but without any amazement.

He worked while there was light; then wrapping the idol carefully in soft grasses and leaves and tying it into a parcel with vines he set out to follow the stream by starlight.

Now into the solemn caverns of the wood came rolling solemnly the noise of the ocean. Wafts of sweet scent wandered to him from flowering shrubs whose flowers he could not discern, and large soft moths brushed across his face. He was foot-sore and perhaps sorrowful, and he knew that soon he must quit this island which was so beautiful and romantic under its crown of horror, and go, he knew not whither, but certainly never again to any place like this; but nothing disturbed his enjoyment of the hour. His thoughts were slow and peaceful, and looking up through the trees he saw the heavens without disquiet, although they were eternal. The stream laughed and ran joyously forward to the waterfall. He looked about him and knew where he was. The stream which had borne him such pleasant company was the same whose torrent he had seen wavering and distorted on the night of the earthquake.

He hitched the god a little closer up under his arm and turned into a path he knew. As he neared the village he heard voices not far off. He stopped. Yes, that was Fuma's voice: and the laugh—only Lueli could laugh like that. Standing in the darkness he blessed them. The god weighed on his arm, and it occurred to him that this was the fist time he had ever returned from a walk bringing with him a present for Lueli. Lueli never came back without some gift or other; he was as prodigal as his native clime. Trails of flowers which festooned the doorway and wound themselves round Mr. Fortune's neck whenever he went in or out. Shells, which were casually thrown down on his mat and ran into his sleep when he turned over in the night. Perfectly uneatable shell-fish because they were so pretty, feathers and fantastic ornaments which he wore with gratified embarrassment round his neck. He too had sometimes brought things back with him, but things practical or edible. Never real presents, objects perishable, useless and inconvenient, friendship's tokens, emblems of love, that passion which man, for all his sad conscience and ingenuity, will never be able quite to tame into something useful.

Well, at last he was making some atonement where he had been so remiss. He was a poor hand at presents: an Englishman with a public school training still lurking in his heel, he would never be able with any sort of grace or naturalness to offer garlands of morning-glories or small gay striped crabs. But he was doing his best; he was bringing Lueli a god.

When Lueli came into the hut Mr. Fortune had eaten his supper and was almost asleep.

"Were have you been all day?" enquired Lueli. "I kept on looking for you, and wondering where you had gone. I was growing very anxious, I assure you."

"I have been to the mountain."

"To the mountain?"

"Yes, right to the top of it."

"Oh! did you see the flames and the smoke they talk about? What's it like? Are there a great many flames? Does it make a great noise? Did you feel frightened? I hope you were careful not to fall in. Tell me all about it."

"It is a very impressive sight."

"Well? Go on!"

"I will tell you the rest to-morrow. Now it

218

is time you went to bed. You needn't trouble about Tibby. I've fed her."

He turned over and fell asleep. All night he lay with the idol close against his side.

For three days he worked on it in secret, chipping and scooping and shaving, rubbing it smooth with fine sand, oiling it, treating it as tenderly as a cricket-bat. As he worked, intent and unflurried, strange thoughts concerning it stole into his mind. Sometimes he thought that the man was himself, listening to the parrot which told him how the doom of love is always to be destroying the thing it looks upon. At other times the man seemed to be Christ, and the bird on His wrist the Holy Ghost. In these suppositions there was no part for the dog, save as an adjunct to the design, steadying the base of the composition, and helping it to stand upright. But there was yet a third fancy; and then the man was Lueli, the bird neither parrot nor dove but the emblem of his personality, while the dog was he himself, looking up at Lueli's bird but on trust not to snatch at it or frighten it away.

On the afternoon of the third day the idol was finished. So far it had been his, the creature of his brain, the work of his hands. In an approving look he took his farewell of it, and dismissing it from his care he put it to stand upright on the rock before the hut. Then, moving very quietly, for inside the hut Lueli was taking his afternoon nap and must not be disturbed till everything was ready, he went to the bush by the spring where the red flowers grew. Of these he wove a rather uncouth garland, after the style of the daisy-chains that children make, but a daisy-chain like slow drops of blood. He arranged this round the idol and walked into the hut.

"Lueli!"

Under the smooth brown eye-lids the eyes flickered and awakened. Lueli blinked at him, shut his eyes once more and stretched protestingly. It was all most right: he would hear the words as he should hear them, he would hear them as in a dream.

"Lueli, on the rock outside there is something waiting for you. Go out and see what it is."

He was conscious of Lueli rising and passing him by, and pausing for a moment on the threshold. He sat down with his face to the wall, for he dared not watch an encounter that must be so momentous. Even the eyes of his mind he turned away, and sat in a timeless world, listening. Then, at last, he heard and was released—for what he heard, a murmur, a wandering wreath of sound, was Lueli talking softly to his god.

He made a movement to arise, and then stayed himself. This time he would not intrude, would not interfere. Lueli should be left in peace. He too was at peace, wasn't he? His atonement had been accepted, his part was done. Now there was nothing left for him but to go away. He began to reckon the days. His letter had caught the boat, he knew; for last night the canoe had returned and Moki told him that he had seen the Captain and put the letter into his hands. That was two days ago, and so by now Archdeacon Mason had hitched on his gold-rimmed eyeglasses and was scanning the letter at arm's length in that dignified way he had, a way of reading letters which was as much as to announce: "Whilst reserving my judgment I remain perfectly infallible." At any rate by to-morrow morning he would learn that Mr. Fortune wished to be recalled from Fanua: for though the boat touched at two or three ports before reaching St. Fabien, she was never more than half a day out of her time. By this reckoning the launch might be expected, perhaps to-morrow evening, perhaps on the day following. Then the canoe would push out to the opening of the reef and dodge forward between two waves. He would stand up in the canoe, catch hold of a rope, push against that footing, buoyant and unsteady almost as the sea. He would be on the launch, looking at the neat life-belt, and smelling brass-polish again and warm machine oil. He would be off, he would be gone.

Outside among the birds and the sliding shadows of the palm-fronds Lueli was still talking to his god—a happy noise. Mr. Fortune listened for a minute or two and then went on thinking. He would have no luggage and that was a pity, for he felt the need of doing something business-like, packing would have been a solace. Stay! There would of course be presents: the islanders would not allow him to depart without gifts. They would give him mats, carved bowls and platters, a pig-sticker hung with elaborate tassels, a pipe. A pleasant people, and very beautiful, with their untrammelled carriage and arabesqued nakedness. He glanced down at his forearm where he had allowed old Hina to prick out a vignette of a fish with whiskers. While she was jabbing and chattering he had thought: "A man who has lost his faith in God may perfectly well allow himself to be tattooed." After Lueli, Hina was the islander with whom he had gone nearest to a feeling of intimacy. In extreme old age as in infancy, distinctions of nationality scarcely exist; and Hina had seemed to him very little different from any legendary old lady in an English chimney-corner. She might almost have been his godmother, grown so aged as to be grown gay, and without her wig.

To-morrow he must go round and bid Goodbye to everybody. They would be very surprised, very exclamatory: he did not think that they would be very much upset. If they had seemed rather unreal to him how much more unreal must he have seemed to them! They had been on easy terms with him—they would be on easy terms with anybody; they had accepted his odd ways without demur. While he still preached they had sometimes listened, and when he ceased preaching they asked no questions. When he was happy they smiled back, and when he was parched with anxiety they had not appeared to notice much difference. And at all times they continued to supply him with food and to perform any service he required of them.

They had grown accustomed to him but they had not assimilated him; and his odd ways they had taken as something quite natural since he himself was an oddity. His departure would affect them much as if a star had fallen out of their sky: that is to say it wouldn't really affect them at all. There were once three stars where now you see two: there was once a white man with a magic box which groaned when he trampled it, who came to Fanua. In the course of time the few remaining people who had seen the lost star would brag a little about its superior size and lustre, saying that there were no such stars in these days; and similarly in times to come a black and white being ten foot high and able to speak in a voice of thunder for seven days and seven nights might haunt the groves of Fanua. The ginger-nuts, they too might be commemorated in the fact that he fed men with red-hot pebbles. All he hoped was that they would not use him to frighten children with. But alas!—he was fooling himself. There would soon be plenty of white men to frighten the children of Fanua, to bring them galvanized iron and law-courts and commerce and industry and bicycles and patent medicines and American alarm clocks, besides the blessing of religion. The island could not hope to keep its innocence much longer. Had he not come, a single spy? And soon there would come battalions. Poor islanders! He almost said: "Poor flock!" Well, to-morrow he must bid them good-bye, and to-morrow too, before he bade farewell to the rest he must say: "I am going away, Lueli, I am going away for ever."

And then—*suppose the launch didn't come?* Suppose that the earthquake at Fanua had been but a ripple of an enormous earthquake which had swallowed up St. Fabien?

It would not do to fancy such things. He got up and walked out of the hut. Lueli was gone and had taken his god with him; may be he had carried him off to the little copse where he had cherished the old one. Absently Mr. Fortune sat down on the altar. His hand touched something cold and flabby. It was the garland of red flowers which he had woven in order to give the idol a more festive and Christmas-tree appearance—for a present is a present twice over if it be tied up prettily. He smiled, and hung it round his neck.

He was still sitting on the altar when Lueli

came strolling back for supper. He came singing to himself, and as he walked he tossed a couple of small fish from hand to hand.

"Why didn't you come and bathe too? Look! I caught these in my fingers."

"How beautiful they are!"

They were silvery fish with black and vermilion markings and rose-coloured fins. Their strange blue eyes were yet bright, and they retained the suppleness and shine of life. One does not admire things enough: and worst of all one allows whole days to slip by without once pausing to see an object, any object, exactly as it is.

"We will have them for supper," he said. "I am sorry that I forgot to come bathing. But I'll tell you what. There will be a moon to-night, we might bathe after supper by moonlight. Unless you want to go down to the village."

"No. It would be a lark to bathe."

The night was so mild that after bathing they lounged on the rocks, dangling their legs in the water, which felt even more surprisingly tepid because its black and silver pattern looked so cold. The ledge where they sat was padded with the soft tough growth of sea plants. Out on the reef some gulls were complaining.

The shadow hid his own face but Lueli sat in full moonlight. It was a good moment to speak.

"Lueli, I am going away from Fanua."

There would be no need to add: "I am going away for ever." Somehow, from the tone of his voice or by some curious sympathy, Lueli had guessed. He started so violently that he lost his balance and slipped off the rock. He swam a few strokes out into the pool and then turned and came back again and caught hold of Mr. Fortune's knees to moor himself.

"But if you go you will leave me," he said, lying along the water and looking up into his friend's face. "Don't go!"

"I must, my dear. It is time."

"Are you going back to your own country?"

"Yes. I expect so. Anyhow, I must go. A boat will come for me, the same boat which brought me when I came to the island. Perhaps to-morrow, perhaps the day after."

"Not to-morrow!" Lueli cried out, his face suddenly convulsed with distress.

Mr. Fortune nodded.

"To-morrow or the next day."

"But why do you only tell me now? Now there will be no time to do anything, I can't even make you a pipe. Stay longer! Stay even a little longer! I thought you would stay for ever."

"I'm sorry if I have left it too late. I did it for the best, I didn't want to spoil our last days."

"But when did you know that you would go away?"

"A long time ago. A bird—" He stopped. It would not do to tell Lueli what the bird had said to him. He would not understand, he was incapable of understanding, because he was incapable of feeling that sad, civilized and proprietary love which is anxious and predatory and spoil-sport. Even now despite his distress at hearing that his friend was about to leave him he wasn't attempting to interfere or to do anything about it.

"Lueli, you know how sorry I am to be leaving you. I will not speak of it much, I don't think we need upset each other by telling our feelings. We know them already. But I have one consolation. I am not leaving a weakling, someone that I should have to feel uneasy about. When I think of you, as I shall do constantly,

228

it will be with admiration and confidence."

He looked down at the face raised toward his. Affection, grief, the most entire attention were depicted thereon; but for all these Lueli's countenance still kept its slightly satirical air. And this, because it was the expression most essentially and characteristically his, the aspect that nature had given him, was dearest of all.

"When I came here you were still almost a child. How the three years have changed you! You are as tall as I am now, and a great deal stronger. You are almost as strong as Kaulu whom you used to tell me about—Kaulu the strong boy, who broke the waves with his hands and forced open the jaws of the King Shark who had swallowed his brother. And you are intelligent too, and as you grow older you will become more so. Perhaps you may become as wise and prudent as Kana, who rescued the sun and moon and stars and put them back into the sky. And when he held up the sun the cock crowed. Do you remember telling me that? And as for charm—why, I think you the most popular young man on the island and the best-loved. It delights me to see it."

"You flatter me," answered Lueli in a pleased voice.

229

Then he sighed. "I wish you were not going," he said, "I shall miss you. I shall miss you terribly. Oh, why must you leave me?" And he hung his head, and kicked his heels disconsolately.

The water splashed up, drops of spray fell on Mr. Fortune. He shivered, but it was not the falling spray which chilled him. What could he say, how was he to comfort this child?

"Do you remember how I used to tell you about my God?"

"Yes, of course I remember."

"I haven't spoken of Him lately and perhaps you have noticed that."

"Yes."

"Well, the reaon why I didn't speak of Him was—I have lost Him. I lost Him on the same night that you lost yours, the night of the earthquake. No!"—Lueli had made a sudden movement of enquiry—"He wasn't anything in the hut, He wasn't any of the things that were burnt. He wasn't the kind of God that could be burnt. But He was the kind of God that could perfectly well be lost; and, as I say, I have lost Him."

"But perhaps you will find Him, perhaps He will come back. I—my god——"

Lueli's voice sank into a warm cautious silence, the silence of a lover.

Mr. Fortune put out a hand and stroked the wet head.

"No. I am quite sure I shall never find Him. But I have no doubt He is somewhere around, and that is why I am telling you of my loss. Because, you see, when I go I shall leave Him behind; my God will remain here on the island where I lost Him. And while He remains, a part of me will remain too. I do not leave you utterly."

"Like a keepsake?" ventured Lueli after thinking it over.

"Yes. Like a keepsake. But rather more than a keepsake. Almost like leaving part of myself."

"Yes. I think I understand."

"So now do you feel happier?"

"Not now. But I shall later on."

It had not been anywhere near as bad as he had dreaded that it would be. It had even been a rather comfortable conversation and one that he would be able to look back upon with kindness.

The next day, the last day, was spent in packing and leave-taking. The news of his approaching departure was received with genuine re-

gret, and from everyone he met with such kind
concern that it would have been impossible not
to feel gratified even if he had wished to be
above that sort of feeling. Ori, Teioa and the
other important islanders got up a farewell
feast in his honour. Speeches were made, his
health was drunk, and afterwards Mr. Fortune
sat on the best mats, flushed with praise and
wearing as many garlands as a May Queen or
a coffin, while presentations were made to him.
A necklace of carved sharks-teeth, bracelets of
scented nuts, mother-of-pearl earrings, several
pipes, spears, paddles and carved walking sticks,
rolls of tapa and fine mats, coloured baskets,
polished bowls, sweet-meats and cosmetics, several remembrance-knots of curiously plaited
hair and charms of all sorts—these were piled
up on his lap and all around him. Only Lueli
brought no gift. He sat beside him, examining
and praising the gifts of the others and pointing
out their beauties.

"I do hope he isn't feeling out of it because
he has brought no present," thought Mr. Fortune. "My blessed child, he is too generous to
have anything left to give. But I can't bear to
think that he might be put out of countenance.
I could almost wish——"

At that moment he became aware that Lueli was no longer by his side. The conversation suddenly died down, there was a conscious, premonitory pause and people were looking toward the door of the house. They wriggled to either side, opening a sort of lane. And then Lueli stepped over the threshold, carrying a resplendent head-dress of straw-coloured and scarlet feathers.

Walking solemnly, with a rapt and formal face, he advanced down the lane, bearing on high the softly-waving and coloured crown, till with a deep bow he laid the head-dress at Mr. Fortune's feet.

"But Lueli!" exclaimed Mr. Fortune, too much overcome for words of thanks. "This lovely thing, this marvellous thing! Is it—can it be——?"

"Lueli is your especial friend," said Ori. "It is right that he should make you the best gift."

There was a loud hum of approval. Mr. Fortune raised the head-dress, admired it all round, and put it on. The hum of approval swelled into acclamations and loud cheers.

Then it was Mr. Fortune's turn to produce gifts. He had spent most of the forenoon going

233

over his possessions, such as they were, and in between spells of working on the idol he had contrived to make an assortment of pipe-stoppers, tooth-picks, bodkins and such like small items. With these, and the mother-of-pearl counters and almost all his buttons he was enabled to produce a tolerable array; and though he apologized a great deal over their inadequacy there was no need to apologize, for the recipients were overjoyed with objects so distinguished and far-fetched.

The knife, at once his most personal and valuable possession, was naturally for Lueli, and so was his pipe. Ori received the magnifying glass and his two sons the whistle and the flint-and-steel lighter respectively. To Teioa he presented the magnet and to Mrs. Teioa the medicine spoon. Lueli's mother went into fits of rapture over the measuring tape, Tekea, a handsome, rather taciturn fellow who had helped a great deal with the new hut, was much gratified by the nail-file, the Parnell medal was hung round Fuma's neck and the pencil-case round Vaili's. The pencil sharpener he gave to Lei-lei, village sorceress, doctoress and midwife, who declared that it would be an invaluable asset. At the

234

last moment he remembered Hina, the old story-teller. He gave her the wash-leather bag.

After songs and dances the party broke up at a late hour; and still wearing his crown Mr. Fortune walked home with Lueli by moonlight. The other gifts he had left behind, for Ori had undertaken to see that they were packed properly, ready for the morrow. A night-bird was calling among the trees—a soft breathy note like an alto flute—and the roof of the hut shone in the moonlight.

"Will you go on living here, Lueli?"

"Of course. Where else should I like to live so well?"

"I am glad. I shall know how to picture you when I am thinking of you."

"When I think of you I shall not know where you are."

"Think of me here."

As a result of the party they overslept themselves, and they were still breakfasting when Tekea came running up to say that the launch had been sighted. Mr. Fortune became a man of action. He knew instantly that no one from St. Fabien could be allowed to set foot on his island. He gave instructions to Tekea accordingly: a canoe might go out to the reef to keep them in play, but no one was to be taken off the launch on any account.

"What shall I tell them," asked Tekea: "if they want to land?"

"Tell them—" What could they be told? Small-pox, tigers, taboos, hornets in swarm; he ran over a few pretexts but nothing seemed quite suitable. "Tell them," he said, "tell them I say so. By the way, you might take them out a few bananas."

Tekea grinned. He was an understanding fellow. He ran back to the village while Mr. Fortune and Lueli followed at a more leisurely pace. There was nothing to delay them: Mr. Fortune was already dressed in his European clothes, and the feather head-dress was carefully packed in a large leafy frail. Just as they were crossing the dell he stopped. "Wait a minute," he said, "we never washed up the breakfast things."

"I can do that afterwards."

"No, indeed! That would be dismal. We will do it now, and shake out the mats. There is plenty of time, and if there isn't it won't hurt them to wait. They'll have the bananas to amuse them."

Together they put all straight and tidy, folded up Mr. Fortune's island clothes, threw away the garlands of overnight and the unused twigs and vines that had been plucked for the packing of the head-dress, and removed every trace of departure. Then they set forth for the village once more.

Everyone was out to see Mr. Fortune off and wish him good-luck. The launch was outside the reef and his luggage was being conveyed on board. There was a vast amount of it and it seemed even more numerous because of the quantity of helping hands outstretched to deal with it. It was all so exactly like what he had foreseen that he felt as though he were in a dream: the beach, the lagoon, thronged with excited well-wishers, canoes getting their outriggers entangled and nearly upsetting, hands thrust out of the water to right them, everyone laughing and exclaiming. Everyone that is, except Lueli: Mr. Fortune had not been able to include him in his foreseeing of the last act. He had been lively and natural at breakfast; but now he was silent, he was pale, he was being brave. "If I say something cheerful," thought Mr. Fortune: "I may upset him. What shall I say?" At the water's edge he turned to him.

"Forgive me if—" He got no further for Lueli's arms were flung about his neck. Mr. Fortune gently patted him on the back.

He got into the canoe and the dream began again. The canoe manœuvred at the opening of the reef, it dodged forward between the waves. He stood up, he felt the sea sidle and thrust under him as the earth had done on the night of the earthquake, the rope was thrown, he touched the side of the launch, he was on board.

In the launch was the Secretary, grown bald and corpulent, who immediately began to tell Mr. Fortune about the Great War, saying that the Germans crucified Belgian children, were a disgrace to humanity, and should be treated after the same fashion themselves.

Mr. Fortune sat listening and saying at intervals "Indeed," and: "How terrible!" and: "Of course I have heard nothing of all this." His eyes were fixed upon the coral reef where Lueli stood, poised above the surf, and waving a green frond in farewell. As the launch gathered speed Lueli's figure grew smaller and smaller; at last he was lost to sight, and soon the island of Fanua appeared to be sinking back into the sea whence it had arisen.

Now the secretary was abusing the French; and from them he passed to the Turks, the Italians and King Ferdinand of Bulgaria. Mr. Fortune could not yet gather who was fighting who, still less what they were all fighting about. However there seemed no doubt but that it was a very comprehensive dog-fight.

"Shall I go back to Europe?" he thought. "I couldn't fight but perhaps I might pick up the wounded. No! I am too old to be of any use; and besides, I have no money to pay my passage."

The launch scurried on with a motion that might have been described as rollicking if it had not also been so purposeful and business-like. The paint which used to be white picked out with dark blue was now buff picked out with chocolate. The mechanic was a new one. He had stared at Mr. Fortune when the latter came aboard, and now he came out of the engine house with a rag in his hand and began polishing the brass-work, turning round at frequent intervals to have another look at him.

"Perhaps he expected me to carry a goatskin umbrella," thought Mr. Fortune.

The Secretary displayed no such interest. He asked no questions about Fanua, a negligible peaceful spot, not like Europe, not to be com-

pared to St. Fabien, where there was a gun-boat
and a fermenting depot for the Red Cross Fund.
And as for Mr. Fortune he had known years
ago all that there was to know about him and
that wasn't much.

His conversation shifted from the wife of an
ex-prime minister who was certainly in the pay
of the Germans to the proprietor of the Pension
Hibiscus who had attempted to charge for teas
served to the ladies of the Swab Committee and
was probably a spy. Meanwhile the island of
Fanua was sinking deeper into the Pacific
Ocean.

At last he stopped talking. Mr. Fortune knew
that he ought now to say something but he felt
incapable of comment. He did not seem to have
an idea left. Everything that was real, everything that was significant had gone down with
the island of Fanua and was lost for ever.

No. After all there was one thing he might
ask, one small interest which had been overlooked in the pillaging of his existence.

"By the by, can you tell me the exact time?"

He was an hour and twenty minutes out. A
bad guess on his part. But perhaps it was not
quite such bad guessing as it now appeared to
be; for he had spent three and a half years in

Fanua, and his watch might well have lost half an hour or so in that time. It was a good watch once; but Time will wear out even watches, and it had seen its best days.

ENVOY

My poor Timothy, Good-bye! I do not know what will become of you.